CANYON

CHRISTOPHER J. HOLCROFT

CANYON

CHRISTOPHER J. HOLCROFT

DoctorZed
Publishing
www.doctorzed.com

This third edition published 2022 by DoctorZed Publishing.

DoctorZed Publishing books may be ordered through booksellers or by contacting:

DoctorZed Publishing
10 Vista Ave
Skye, South Australia 5072
www.doctorzed.com
61-(0)8 8431-4965

ISBN: 978-0-6455442-5-1 (sc)
ISBN: 978-0-6455442-6-8 (e)

A CIP number for this book is available at the National Library of Australia.

Cover image moutaineer © Yanlev | Dreamstime.com

Printed in Australia, UK & USA

DoctorZed Publishing rev. date: 11/07/2022

To my wife Yvonne,
for all her everlasting love.

To youth everywhere…
believe in yourself and train for the disasters you
don't want to happen.

"Remember, if you ever need a helping hand, you'll find one at the end of your arm … As you grow older, you will discover that you have two hands. One for helping yourself, the other for helping others.»

Audrey Hepburn.

Chapter One

Slowly William inched his way backwards on the rock shelf. The bluewater rope ran tightly through his abseil rack. The teenager slid the rope protector in place to stop the rope abrading on the edge of the rock face. He shifted his legs shoulder width apart and leant backwards.

His right hand held the rope under his bottom and his left hand was forward of the metal abseiling rack around the rope. William took up the slack in the rope and stepped down to the first level. He moved his feet together and over balanced sending him into a mini free fall.

"Got you!" Scott yelled from the bottom of the cliff as he tightened his grip on William's abseil rope and leant backwards.

Scott 'married' the end of the rope with the main part of the abseil rope and tightened his grip. He was belaying William when he saw his mate slip. His quick action averted a possible major problem by tightening the abseil rope. The youth's action locked the rope in William's abseil gear and prevented him from moving down the rope.

"Hey William, open your legs shoulder width apart again and lean back," Scott said. "I'll lower you back on the cliff."

Scott then eased back on the rope to allow more slack and for William to take control.

"Thanks, Scott. I misjudged my footing."

Scott watched William intently and allowed him free play with the rope. William sat on his haunches, corrected his position and then kicked out from the cliff. The movement sent the teenager out and down in a controlled abseil. The sound of 'clunk, clunk' of heavy boots hitting the ground echoed at the base of the cliff as William landed. Scott dropped his part of the rope to allow William more slack to feed it through his abseil equipment.

"Of course, you know I was only testing you up there," William said with a cheesy grin.

"Of course – I'm the official Unit tester when I belay."

William divested himself of the rope from his equipment and walked over to Scott. He picked up the rope and curled it around his waist and married the ends. It was an automatic gesture as each of the boys in the Venturer Unit took turns in belaying after abseiling.

"Who's next?" Scott asked.

"Peter's up next followed by Mark and Ian," William said as he craned his neck upwards to see if Peter had started to hook onto the rope.

"I'll head on up," Scott said. "I'll also ask Mike if he's willing to let us do some face first or Forward Geneva today."

"Good on you, Scott. We haven't done any of that for some time. Cheers."

Scott made his way across the nicely mowed sports ground and climbed the hilly embankment. The abseil area was on top of a former rock quarry, long abandoned. The quarry itself had been flattened out and public tennis courts and a car park had been built. The local Council knew Venturer Units and other groups used the quarry for adventurous activity but did nothing to hamper them. A series of homes backed onto the top of the quarry.

Scott turned the corner and saw Mike, his Venturer Leader, talking with one of the Venturers and explaining to him how to adjust his harness. Mike was an Army Reserve Captain who loved being involved with youth when he was not in the army.

"Good one, Scott," Mike said without looking up.

"That was a good save with William."

Scott was slightly taken back. Does this man miss anything in relation to what the Venturers did, he thought?

"No problems. Will just lost his footing for a moment. Well, he was just testing me, he said," Scott said with a smirk on his face.

"Sure, he was ... now I bet he wants to do Forward Geneva? Would I be right?"

"Actually, I was going to ask if we could do some Forward Geneva," Scott said.

"Once Ian has gone down, we'll start the face first jumps. I want to ensure everyone has had at least one jump backwards before we do any forwards work."

"Okay. I'll let the others know," Scott said as he continued walking towards the other Venturers.

Scott joined in with the other boys as they discussed abseil options and the thrill of running face first down the cliff.

"It wrenches your gut but is sheer exhilaration," Ian said.

"Yeah, but if you don't keep running you pay for it next day with a sore stomach," Peter chimed in.

Mike had finished adjusting the new Venturer's abseil harness and walked over to the rest of the boys. He was proud of the way they listened to instruction and heeded advice. Mike had arranged a month ago for his Venturer Unit to visit some Army Reserve Commandos and for them to instruct the boys on the finer points of rappelling – or abseiling. This included Forward Geneva. The Commandos used their rappelling to generally get to their enemy quicker down a cliff. However, the soldiers also carried weapons, wore webbing and had loads of special equipment. Mostly, the boys would be lucky to even carry backpacks on an abseil.

"Once we have all done Forward Geneva it will be time to concentrate on our rescues again," Mike said. "We've got the canyoning trip coming up over the long weekend in a few months' time and I want to ensure you are all up to speed."

Ian shifted in his stance.

"If most of us know how to rescue, what's the issue?" Ian asked as he lifted his right hand to shield his eyes from the sun.

Mike looked at him but re-directed the question. "Who can help Ian here?"

"If anyone has a problem on the rope in the canyon it will be a major rescue effort to get people out," Peter said.

"What if you were second last and hit your head on the way down? You really would want the last person to know how to rescue you, wouldn't you?"

Ian looked at Peter and quickly realised the error of what he had said.

"Maybe it's time to tell you about the teenage boy who died at Julia Falls," Mike said. "Tell Will to join us, Peter."

The boys waited for Will to climb the small hill and work his way around the top of the cliff to join them.

"Grab a seat and have a listen and you'll understand why I've pushed for a lot of extra training for you in abseiling with the Commandos and here." The boys knew when Mike talked like this he was out to try and protect them. "Two Venturer-age boys went to a large set of waterfalls called Julia Falls for some abseiling," Mike said.

"The falls are in the Blue Mountains area west of Sydney and surrounded by pretty rugged terrain. The boys had to abseil down three faces before the river opened out into a wide flat rocky area. It ended abruptly at Julia Falls which had a drop of about the equivalent of a 25-storey building.

"One of the boys threw the rope over the falls after securing one end. Both looked over the edge and thought they saw the rope reaching the bottom. Instead, it was knotted about 12 metres down under a small ledge. One of the boys went over the edge and started abseiling but got caught up in the rope knot. He didn't know how to tie off, disentangle himself and continue. Also, he didn't know how to prussick or climb back up the cliff to safety on the rope."

Not a word was being muttered by the boys as they sat quite attentively to Mike. He continued.

"When the boy became stuck it sent the other one into a panic as he couldn't pull his mate up the cliff and over the edge for safety – it was just too hard."

Ian couldn't hang on any longer.

"Why couldn't the boy on top use some karabiners like a pulley and haul his mate up over the edge?"

"When you go unconscious or die, the weight on the rope is extreme. There was just no way physically, the boy on top could pull his mate up … he needed winches and pulleys and a lot of engineering type experience to bring it all together.

"The boys neither had the experience nor the equipment to effect any major rescue of each other. So, the stuck boy just sat there tangled next to the waterfall with water spray constantly blowing onto him from the chilly winds that occasionally whip through the valley. The second boy went back for help, but this took several hours to climb out where he could raise the alarm. Then it took several hours for rescuers to reach the stuck boy. The second boy was dead when rescuers arrived," Mike said.

"What did he die of?" Scott asked.

"He died of hyperthermia where the constant spray of the water and wind chill from the valley cooled his body to the point where it killed him," Mike said as his voice had a noticeable change in it.

"Couldn't the boy on top use his mobile phone to call for help?"

"No. This accident happened before mobiles were really in fashion. Even still, with today's technology, we still have problems getting emergency services to help us when we have misadventure. It's not that they won't help, it's just a lack of proper co-ordination on our part as a youth organisation and being able to share information to properly identify who is to be rescued, exactly what maps were the people using, their escape routes and so on.

"My aim is to ensure you can enjoy the challenges of the activity you choose to do and that if anything happens to you,

you are self-reliant enough to get out of most problems or can get your mate out."

There was a noticeable few seconds quiet as Mike's words sunk in to each boy. Scott listened intently. He was always hearing of people being rescued and their lack of preparedness by his father. Scott's father Allan was a Police Officer and would hear about the various rescues from other Police Officers and then tell his wife Kelly when he got home.

"We'll be going near Julia Falls for our canyoning weekend away, so we need to be prepared," Mike said.

Peter looked at the other Venturers and took the initiative. 'Okay, we've heard our story for the day. It is a true one and it shows why we must train hard – so we can play hard, as our Commando friends kept reminding us," Peter said. "Who's next?" he continued as he stood up.

A huge grin came over Ian. "Actually, Mr Chairman, you are," Ian said.

The rest of the boys laughed as they stood up, ready to resume their abseiling. The preparation for the canyoning trip also included some days of basic rock climbing for the Venturers. Their expertise in rope handling, rope calls and descent were now noticeable.

Instead of a verbal remonstration from each other if there was a problem, a mere look from any affected Venturer to his mate sufficed. On one Thursday meeting night the Unit went indoor rock climbing to hone their skills. Mike motioned to Peter as the pair watched most of the boys in the Unit try the various climbing routes on the man-made walls.

"There is now calm among the boys and an expectation to perform at a high level," Mike said.

"Yeah – they've come a long way in a short time. But then again, not every Venturer Unit can call on the Commandos for extra tuition."

Mike looked Peter straight in the eye. "A lot of the Commandos were former Venturers, which is why they were also keen to help out in their spare time," Mike said. "Who knows, maybe someone from our Unit may want to take the challenge of going for a green beret and becoming a Commando themselves one day."

Peter smiled. "You weren't intentionally recruiting for the Army Reserve, were you?' he asked.

"No. I was just introducing a new dimension in service to the community and thoughts about possible career lines for the boys. It would be wrong for me to push them into the army ... but not to expose them to it!"

Peter recounted the excitement and thrill the Venturers had felt when they visited the Commandos at their Army base south of Sydney. He said the boys were particularly thrilled not only to abseil the special abseil wall but also try out the Blackhawk helicopter simulator and crawl over the mock helicopter shell set up in a special warehouse type building.

"Abseiling is great, but I bet you can't replace the thrill of the Blackhawk?" Peter asked Mike.

"No. The Army air taxi has an adrenalin push all of its own. Hopefully you'll never have to fly in one for real."

Chapter Two

The following Thursday night the Venturers again visited the indoor climbing centre as part of their Unit meeting.

The boys paired off, with one attached to a belay line bolted to the floor and the other hooked on to the rope ready to climb the walls. Fake man-made rocks of various shapes, sizes and colours were bolted to the walls. Climbers negotiated their way to the ceiling via set rock colours. Only a few climbers made it upside down on the wall hanging on with their fingertips and wedging their feet against the rocks. Most people 'fell' while they tried to climb these last sections.

"Hey Mike, do you think I'll make it," Ian asked.

Mike looked up to see Ian on the ceiling, about to go upside down in a daring move to reach the hardest area of the climbing wall. He gave Ian a 'thumbs up' and watched quietly while the deft teenager pitted his strength and cunning against the wall. Ian wedged his left foot firmly against one rock, arched his back so he was pressing against the ceiling and then reached forward for the next rock.

It was all over in a millisecond but was watched in slow motion by Mike and Peter. Ian lost his footing and started to yell 'falling' when Brett married his belay ropes and held on tight, locking any movement of Ian. The 'falling' Venturer only fell around a metre before the belay took hold and his body jerked and came to a stop. Ian looked more like a spider hanging onto a strand of web as he was blown in a few different directions by the wind.

"Nice try, Ian. Good catch Brett. Great teamwork boys," Mike said.

Mike Hunter was not a rock climber. He could abseil, rescue and descend canyons, but hated the thought of climbing up rock walls and over ledges, hundreds of metres from the ground. He encouraged rock craft within his Unit as a way to help the Venturers dispel many of their fears. Abseiling was a great way to instil confidence and build trust between the Venturers. It also created opportunities for leadership.

Mike's day job was a newspaper journalist for an afternoon paper called *The Daily Globe*. He was a police rounds reporter who covered the seamy side of life from murders, robberies and tragic accidents. The last thing he wanted was for his Venturers to become another news statistic.

Also, Mike knew Police already showed their 'personal' views in the Media that the only ones good enough to do anything adventurous in the community and the best prepared, were the Police. Mike found the same cops saying the same things about groups of adventurers who had misfortune hit them.

"More care should be taken. They should have been better prepared and trained before setting out ...." Police would tell the Media. He was determined not to have the same thing be said about him if anything happened to his Venturers.

Scott had teamed up with one of the Rovers, a more experienced teenager aged 19 who left the Unit a year ago. Cameron Wagstaff had been a good mentor to Scott and the pair got on famously well. While Scott was still gangly with a shock of blonde hair and green eyes, Cameron was the opposite. He was tall, well chiselled, had dark hair and brown eyes. His hands dwarfed Scott's. Cameron had become an apprenticed plumber and was quite adept now at using his strength. He was also a keen rock climber and started to teach Scott some of the basic body moves and techniques.

"This is called bouldering," Cameron said to an attentive Scott. "You reach up to the first level of handhelds on a rock climb and take your weight. Then, gently lift upwards, lower your body and reach upwards again to the next level of handhelds."

Scott looked up in shock. Cameron had seemed to magically pull himself up from one level to the next while his feet were off the ground. The concentration on Cameron's face was extraordinary. Every muscle in his body seemed to have flexed as he lowered his body and would then lift his weight only using his fingers. A huge veil of concentration descended on Cameron as he propelled his body up to the next level of man-made rocks. He hung there for a few seconds allowing his adrenaline to subside. Cameron's body went limp, and he let go of the rocks and fell to the floor.

"Wow! That was great," Scott said. "Did it take you long to perfect the moves?"

"Yeah, I was introduced to bouldering by Mike when I was

a Venturer. I liked pitting myself against myself – well at least there's no competition, is there?"

"That was truly amazing," Scott said. "I don't think I'll ever become that good."

Cameron looked closely at Scott. For a few milliseconds that seemed like minutes, he saw his life as a Venturer come back into focus. He too, had struggled to learn how to master his body and push it to extremes.

"You don't know what you are capable of doing until you try ... and I mean really try," Cameron said. "I also know what it is like to be out of shape and out of practice. If I miss a week of bouldering, I really feel the pressure next time I step up to the walls for a climb."

Scott had a go at climbing the wall. He stayed within a set colour pattern of rocks and slowly inched his way upwards. Cameron advised which way to proceed if the younger boy became stuck. On Scott's left an older teenager made his way shakily up the rock wall. Below, his friend belayed but was distracted by someone else talking to him.

Scott could see it coming but could not stop the fall. The teenager was three-quarters up the wall when he lost his footing. He had yelled to his friend to take up the slack of the rope – but to no avail. His mate was too engaged in conversation to hear. The teenager had teetered on the edge of some rock foot holds, shaking with fear. His legs were vibrating, almost spasmodically. The boy closed his eyes and fell.

Out of instinct, Scott reached out to try and grab the other boy but missed. The teenager fell almost to the giant thick mats on the ground before his partner stopped him. The sudden jolt of his body was painstaking to watch as his friend jerked his belay line taught. The contorted facial expressions said it all. The verbal exchange that followed was not pleasant either.

Scott relaxed once he saw the teenager was safe. He listened intently to Cameron and kept reaching, lifting, and climbing his way to the ceiling. Once at the top, Scott looked down at Cameron who was looking directly back at him.

"Okay Scott, are you ready?" Cameron asked.

"Yep."

"Okay. Let go. I've got you."

Scott let go of the hand holds and pushed away from the rock wall. He fell a few centimetres before Cameron's grip on the rope took hold and he was lowered to the ground.

"Well done, Scott. You looked around before you climbed each step to ensure you had good leverage to push yourself up to the next level," Cameron said. "Don't be afraid to use the tips of your fingers or the tips of your toes to hold on in these controlled areas. After all, if you fall, you should be belayed by your other Venturers."

Scott reached the mats and started to unhook the rope from his abseil equipment.

"The only hassle would be if the Venturers were like some others, we've seen tonight who kept talking to their mates and taking their eye off their partners," Scott said.

"Yeah, in the real world of rock climbing the lack of attention by you or your mates could result in a nasty death or injury."

The boys walked to the adjoining wall section to join Mike, the other Venturers and Rovers.

"Hey Scott, you'll have to try this upside view of the world," Ian yelled out.

Scott followed the sound of the voice and looked up to the ceiling. Ian was again hanging on to any rock hold he could while he pushed his arched back to the ceiling. He made one last concerted effort to touch a bell positioned on the ceiling. A tinkling sound rung out before the youth's belayer heard the magic words 'falling' and Ian started his descent to the mats. The huge Cheshire cat grin on the youth said it all.

"Well done, Ian," Mike started to say as a chorus of Venturers chimed in.

"We knew you'd say that," Peter said as he looked at the other boys who were all laughing.

Scott looked around and noticed the Rovers were becoming animated in their conversations with each other and walked closer to hear what they were saying. He noticed a fourth Rover aged about 20 with a ginger beard and moustache had joined the group and was getting quite loud.

"They shouldn't have died. I've said this all along. If there were more rescue units in the Blue Mountains and other places, they and others like them, probably would be alive today," he said. Cameron joined in and started raising his voice too.

"You're wrong. The rescue units these days are trained for removing trees from houses that have blown down in storms or releasing people from car wrecks – not canyon, caving and other adventure sports that turn into disasters," Cameron said.

"No. There are some rescue units in the Police, Ambulance and State Emergency Services that can handle awkward rescues like large canyons or inside tricky caves."

The exchange started to attract several the other climbers and the Rovers took their cue and agreed to disagree with each other and leave their exchange until another time at another place.

Scott was taken aback by the conversation. Like most people, he thought if someone has a problem through misadventure there were plenty of well-trained people in the government or community to help rescue people in trouble. He became worried. He asked Cameron for some more details.

"What's worse," Ian said, "is that mobile phone reception is not always good in the rugged areas where we seek our adventure.

"Authorities still want us to carry our emergency rescue beacons or EPIRBS with us, wherever we go. Then when we set them off when something happens, it takes forever for the right information to be found about us, what we are doing, where we are doing it etc."

A cold shiver took hold of Scott as he tried to fathom what Cameron had just told him. "Is an EPIRB one of those blinking lights that acts as a radio distress beacon or something?" Scott asked.

"Yeah, when you get into trouble you set it off and a distress signal is sent to the nearest satellite and then relayed to the main emergency centre in Canberra. An EPIRB is an Emergency Position-Indicating Radio Beacon. The problem, is that by the time authorities work out what may be happening and organise local Police, it could take hours … time is very precious in an emergency."

"Don't we have anything in Scouting that can help mobilise

the right people to do the right job with the right gear if there is an incident? After all, we do put a lot of paperwork into our Scout groups before we actually do any adventurous activity."

"No. You must remember Scouting is mainly voluntary. Yes, we have a system where we notify the leaders of our groups where we are going, when we are due back, routes in and out etc ... But if something happens it still takes a long time to bring it all together and actually have rescue people get to us."

Scott had an idea and couldn't wait to get home and discuss it with his Police Inspector father Allan. He started to think of the Rovers and the rescue people he had seen on TV during disasters. Pages of the internet he had casually scanned when looking up Rovers came hauntingly in focus. Hanging in the back of his mind was what Mike had said at abseiling and the death of the teenager like him because of lack of training, extra preparedness, and something else to bring help quickly.

Allan Morrow was making a cup of tea for both he and his wife Kelly when Scott arrived home. The teenager quickly started talking about what the Rovers had said that night and Mike earlier at the abseil day.

"The real problem is the lack of training for when misadventure occurs," Allan told Scott. "Too often the Police Rescue Squad and the State Emergency Services or SES, are called in to help our weekend warrior friends who do a little bit of training and a lot of adventure without the right back-up."

"That's precisely my point," Scott said as he sat in an armchair opposite his father. "What if organisations like

Venturers or Rovers did more training with the Police and set up their own rescue units? Would that work?"

"It could. However, it would be more for the Rover age group of people in their late teens to mid-20s because of the physical strength required. Also, you need to have some life experience and ability to adapt to some pretty trying times"

"Like what?"

"Like gearing up and rushing to a rescue only to find the person died some hours before you reached them. Then it becomes a retrieval."

"Okay. But it could work if the right resources were available, and the right kind of people conducted the rescues."

"Scott, you are forgetting one thing. It takes a long time for Police to find out who has gone missing from where, what they took, learn their experience and if there were any escape routes.

"Then, Police have to organise teams of rescuers from within their own ranks, specialist rescue organisations and the State Emergency Service. It all takes time."

"So, dad if we had scout volunteers in the emergency centres gathering the information before groups went out, would that help?"

A smile broke out across Allan's face as he realised how deeply his son had started to think of the complex problem.

"Yes. The scout volunteers would have to ensure their system of notification was standard with all the right information Police and other emergency workers would need. It would be a major co-ordination effort and need a lot of political assistance to make it happen."

"Ahh. What about if we had both scout volunteers at the emergency centres and well-trained groups of Rovers who could go to the aid of Scouts and others who had problems on cliffs, in caves and even lost in the bush?"

"It would take a lot of setting up. It could be done but would need some good political clout to make it happen. Also, the Rovers would have to virtually become as qualified as Police. I don't think the Police would want them as they might get in the way of any other Police work."

Scott went to bed but could hardly sleep. His mind kept turning over what his father and Cameron had said that night. "There had to be a way to ensure all the scouting people who tried adventure as part of their award schemes could be made safer," he thought to himself.

"There is still a missing ingredient …."

Scott threw the bedclothes off, got out of bed and turned on his bedroom light. He sat at his desk and started writing down his ideas and searching the internet for the pages that kept coming back to him in his mind's eye.

"Found you, at last," Scott said to himself. He kept scrolling through his search engine at the various listings. A swag of volunteer emergency rescue squads comprising Rovers had been trained by Canadian Police and other organisations. The Rovers had then set up their own rescue organisations modelled on their parent organisation that trained them. It was a system that worked. Rovers of all ages were contributing to the Canadian society in a big way to live up to their motto of Service! Scott was keen to bounce his ideas off someone else but had to wait as it was now after midnight and the next school day was only hours away. Morning couldn't come quick enough for Scott. He messaged Mike on his mobile phone before breakfast asking for a contact within the State Emergency Service.

Mike gave him the name and number of Steven King who was an educational officer with the organisation. The hours passed slowly for Scott and finally at 3:10 pm the bell went and school was over for the day. Scott rushed home on his bicycle and rang Steven King to bounce his ideas off him.

Between talking with his father, Cameron and King, Scott felt he had an answer to the emergency conundrum. Scott had searched the internet to firm up his ideas and found the answer in Canada. His job now was to sell his idea and see whether it was a worthwhile proposal that Australians might embrace. It was a big task. He again spoke with his dad to tell him of his ideas and refine his proposals. Next step was to talk with Mike and see what he thought as he had pretty close links with Rovers. Mike was at work when he received Scott's call and listened intently to what his young charge proposed.

"It could work and would be very effective," Mike said. "Your proposal would need some fleshing out but if we can get some government support it could work.

"This is also a good story Scott. I'll talk with my paper's Chief of Staff and see whether I can take it on and do a feature on it and see where it goes and the sorts of responses we receive."

Once Scott heard Mike say it was a good story Scott knew he could be on a winner with his project. It took three days before the story broke in *The Daily Globe* newspaper. Mike had spoken with Rovers from each of the State groups; Emergency Services Ministers and rescue groups from his own State and those in Canada where Scott had drawn his idea.

The story called for the formation of Rover volunteer groups to assist with the manning of a special telephone number '*1 900 scout*'. This was only to be used in emergencies by scouts in trouble. The number was also to be linked to the existing 112 mobile phone emergency number used throughout Australia. Rescue groups were asked to sponsor Rover Crews who wanted to train with them and Police to hone and extend their skills. The Rover Crews would have to undertake specific rescue training and be tested at a high level. Once accredited, they would be able to assist Police and other rescue organisations as an adjunct and independent body.

Talk back radio picked up on the idea and started running with it. Several Emergency Service personnel from Canada were interviewed and extolled how positive the idea of Rovers assisting them was having positive effects in communities everywhere.

TV stations then followed both Mike's story and the radio talk backs to present their packaged stories. This included hapless victims who had been lost or fell off cliffs or got stuck in caves. Invariably, a young fresh-faced Rover was interviewed, and the question rose: "Does it really work having the Rover rescue organisations?"

Always the answer was a resounding 'yes' because they had been trained by the various emergency services and then certified when they reached a particular standard. Safety was the key and service was the deliverer.

Prime Minister Robert Anthony had read Mike's original story and heard the talk back radios. When he saw the TV story he was moved by the simplicity of the plan. It was also a great way to get in touch with new voters aged 18 and over and assist them to focus on giving service to the community. The Prime Minister decided to put his weight behind the scheme and said the emergency centres manned federally would be asked to investigate the viability of Scott's proposal. The Premier of Scott's home state of New South Wales was not going to be outdone either. He ordered his Emergency Services Minister to check out whether the Police, SES and community rescue groups could take on the Rovers and train them up to handle the arduous remote rescues. Rover Crews initially thought the story was a 'beat up' by Mike. Within a few days Mike's story had been published in all states by sister mastheads from his newspaper's parent organisation. Both radio and TV stations also broadcast the stories throughout their national networks. A ground swell of support soon gathered from Rover Crews across all States who were looking for a more meaningful role to play in the community.

A number of Rovers had joined emergency organisations as part of their service. Now they had an opportunity to adopt their own special knowledge of scouting and the various adventure sports and apply it to an enhanced rescue training regime if something more meaningful could be set up. This would help with more community knowledge of who Rovers were and what other roles they could play to help society enjoy the outdoors more safely.

Scott was flummoxed when he saw that Mike's paper had

run with the story over a couple of days. Support from Rover Crews across the country started pouring into the emergency rescue centre in Canberra for Rovers to be trained in what to do and to start organising rosters of people to monitor calls.

The Federal Communications Minister Bill Egan announced the government would commit to setting up the '1 900 scout' hotline within a month if scouts were prepared to staff and operate the emergency centre and work closely with emergency services personnel on an ongoing basis.

New South Wales Police Minister Grant Delaney was the first State Minister to follow suit by saying discussions were taking place between Rover Crews, Police, and emergency services personnel to train the Rover Crews to assist with rescue duties in some remote areas.

The Police Superintendent in charge of the New South Wales Rescue Division was cautious in welcoming the move by the State and Federal Governments to back the Rovers in becoming better trained and more able to assist Police and other emergency services. He was keen to promote the awareness for more organisations like Scouts to have well prepared and trained personnel to assist their own members who may befall any misadventure. However, he was dubious as to whether the Rovers would continue their training and said so in an opposition newspaper to Mike's.

Scott had fielded a number of telephone calls from Rovers across the country in response to Mike's story. When the Police Rescue Superintendent's story was published the web and telephone chatter between Rovers intensified. Cameron went around to see Scott and his parents to discuss the proposed scheme. He could see why the Police seemed sceptical but wanted to talk to Allan Morrow about it.

"So how come the Police aren't coming directly onboard with us and backing our move for better training and organisation for times of misadventure?" he asked Allan.

"It's not that we're not backing you as the Rovers directly, but we have to be cautious. We have to ensure this is not just pie in the sky talk groups of young people are engaged in but that it will actually be carried out at a level Police and other emergency services will accept."

"Allan, have you seen the Canadian model where the Rovers have started their own rescue groups? They actually specialise in areas like caving, bushwalking, canyoning and abseiling."

"No, I haven't had to look at these things before, but I bet there are a lot of cops doing it now. After all, a huge number of police are former Scouts and Girl Guides."

"Once we are up and running properly, Scott's idea will grow like a bushfire. It should then be like a continuous moving wall of training for the upcoming Rovers from Venturers to take part as Crews become registered rescue groups."

"Don't be too worried about the Police. There is a huge groundswell of support for what the Rovers are planning. They just have to reach a high standard; prove they are willing to commit to the long haul and be seen by their peers as being up to the standards required. Once the first crews are trained and blooded with a successful operation, support should be unequivocal.

"I've received quite a few calls at work and many e-mails

from police both in this State and elsewhere congratulating Scott on his proposal and saying they will back the Rovers. Now the ball is rolling, you should ensure the Rovers know the force is generally with them."

"That's what I wanted to hear. I'll go and spread the word quietly. Thanks for your help."

Cameron's face had lit up with Allan's last words and he hurriedly made his exit from the Morrow household so he could start communicating with his Rover Crew and get them to begin spreading the news. The words 'The Force is generally with us' started hitting cyberspace within the hour and emanated from Cameron's computer. Text messages were being sent around the State to encourage the Rover Crews to become fully committed behind Scott's scheme. Canadian Rover Crews were contacted to add their weight and to relay their experiences to their Australian counterparts. A couple of Sydney based Rover Crews were able to elicit support for a couple of Canadian rescue Rovers to be brought to Australia for interviews and to share their experiences so weight could be added to Scott's idea. Crews were encouraged to seek local Media support to encourage other people in the Rover age group to join in and take the bold step in improved training methods.

Scott's local newspaper, the *Peak Gazette*, wanted to promote the burgeoning rescue scheme and arranged a photo of Scott with Cameron, some Rovers and members of the local State Emergency Service and Police.

Allan and Kelly Morrow were pleased with their son and his efforts to help others. However, their ire was raised by the number of phone calls that started to trickle into the house from Venturers and Rovers who wanted more information about the rescue scheme.

"If that phone rings just one more time for Scott I'll have the number changed," Kelly said to Allan over tea.

A few minutes later she changed her mind. The phone rang and she was about to become short with the caller but held her tongue.

"Hello, is this Mrs Morrow?"

"Yes."

"Hi ma'am I am Johnathon Gantert, the New South Wales Governor's Private Secretary. Will you accept a call from his Excellency, Major-General Brian McGrath?"

Kelly's face said it all. She turned a bright red colour and frantically waved to Allan to get his attention.

"Yes, thank you Johnathon." A few moments later General McGrath came on the line.

"Hello Mrs Morrow, this is Brian McGrath thank you for taking my call. I just wanted to congratulate you and Allan on the great work Scott has been doing lately with this rescue scheme of his.

"He's a credit to us all really. I saw that when I met you and your family at Government House when I presented Scott with his bravery award and his Queens Scout Award."

"Thanks, General. Scott becomes very strong minded about some things, but he has a heart of gold. Would you like to speak with him?"

"Yes please. I just want to privately congratulate him on the work he has done to help others and to rally more support for the training of our young people to undertake rescue duties. This sort of operation could save lives and allow many people to explore our rugged country knowing there is a good safety net around them."

Kelly gave the phone to Allan after telling him who was on the line. She then went to Scott's bedroom where he was completing the day's homework from school.

"Scott, you have a special phone call from someone you met at Government House," Kelly said as she watched Scott's face for any expression. The youth looked blankly for a moment and then asked whether the caller was one of the Rovers he had met.

"No. It is General McGrath, the Governor. He wants to have a chat. You better hurry up."

Scott was on his feet like greased lightning and rushed to the phone. His father handed it to him with a giant smile.

"Hi sir, this is Scott."

"G'day Scott I just wanted to privately tell you I am mindful of your efforts I have read about recently in the newspaper.

"You really seem to be living the standard you set when you received your Queens Scout Award. What's more important, is that you have started in motion something others can help the community within times of disaster – not only in this State but across the nation.

"Well done, Scott. I think that was the motto on the sign I saw at Government House with your Venturers."

Scott was almost lost for words and started blushing. He had not sought personal publicity for his scheme but had spoken with his Venturer Leader Mike to bounce the idea off him to see whether he could get the Rovers to do something about it. Instead, Mike took the idea a step further, made it into several feature stories and now it was snowballing across the country and coming to fruition.

"Thanks, sir. I'll always try and do my best. After all, if it helps others in time of need, then we all have succeeded."

Scott rang off. He punched the air and yelled out.

"Eeha. Now things will move."

He was on cloud nine. Both Allan and Kelly put their arms around him as if to drag him back to earth.

"It's not every day the State Governor rings you, or anyone," Allan said.

"Remember Scott. This was a private conversation with the Governor. If the *Peak Gazette*, *The Daily Globe*, or any other news organisation talks with you, the conversation between you and General McGrath cannot be told."

"Yeah, I understand."

Scott floated back to his bedroom. He couldn't focus on his homework. He was too excited.

Chapter Three

The long weekend and the scheduled canyoning trip couldn't come fast enough for Scott and his Venturer Unit. They had trained long and hard; stepped out of their comfort zones with the Commandos and done a number of nights at the indoor rock-climbing centre. They were primed and ready.

The trip to Thomson Canyon, near Alexander in the rugged Blue Mountains of New South Wales, seemed long to Scott and the Venturers. They had all got out of bed sometime around 5 am and made their way to the scout hall just before 6 am to link up. Mike and Cameron drove their cars and took four Venturers each, plus their gear. Mike had divided the various ropes needed for the three abseils into Venturer's packs along with first aid kits and other emergency equipment.

"We'll be going well up into the Blue Mountains to Mount Elizabeth before turning off towards the Zig Zag tourist railway," Mike said in his usual matter of fact way.

"We then hit the dusty roads which lead up to the Alexander Plateau where we'll leave the cars and begin our walk."

The trip through the beautiful Blue Mountains was uneventful. Modern housing soon gave way to old English-style cottages. Small front yards were eclipsed by larger, more spacious frontages. Some parts of the area were directly out of the history books with their unspoilt buildings and cute fences. This all stood in stark contrast to the huge modern monolithic houses being built across Sydney in an urban revival. Hardly any spare ground was left around new homes for lawns and children's play.

"Are you nervous Brett?" Scott asked as he saw his mate wring his hands.

"A bit, it's fine to talk about the fact we're going down some pretty spectacular levels of the valley and doing some great abseils. Even still, I get a bit nervous until I start my descent on a rope."

"Yeah, me too. I guess it would have been better to have seen some films of the area to get a better feel for it, I suppose."

Both boys smiled at each other and raised their hands up and slapped them in a high five movement, American style. They were probably the better abseilers of the Unit and were well watched by the other Venturers. Brett exuded confidence ordinarily, so it was unusual for Scott to see him nervous. The two cars entered a dirt car park at a railway station.

"Where are we?" Ian asked.

"This is Wales Station which is the beginning of the Zig Zag railway," Mike said nonchalantly as he slowed down to drive over the railway tracks.

"Pretty strange name for a railway."

"No. it actually performs a zig zag and travels up and down the mountains in the form of a Z."

Scott couldn't help himself.

"Are you sure Zorro doesn't live around here somewhere?"

"No Scott. Good try. Sometime in the mid-1860s the

railway was built to take produce from Sydney, over the Blue Mountains and beyond," Mike said.

"Trouble was, the mountains were very steep for the locomotives so the engineers built it in the form of a Z so they could climb and descend the mountain easier.

"They have turning areas where the locos could change ends of the train to continue up or down as required. In its day, this railway was considered some sort of engineering feat."

The boys almost felt sated with Mike's local knowledge.

"So where does this dirt track lead us?" Scott asked Mike.

"This is called Coachman's Track and was used by the Cobb and Co stagecoaches in the 1800s to take people to the old shale oil refinery on the other side of Alexander."

Mike smiled.

"Anything else?"

"Yeah, are we there yet?" Brett asked with a smile.

"No. We have another 20 minutes on this dirt road and then we'll be at the start ... eeha."

Mike and Cameron drove the boys through a large pine forest and along the top of a rock peninsula to a car park. Logs added the bush touch to make a formed area to leave the cars. On the other side of the car park was a tourist map on a wooden wall that had a little wooden peaked roof above it. A few large tree trunks had been placed across the service track to prevent cars going any further into the bush. Two metres along the track was a small mailbox type stand that housed a visitor's book. Mike took the book out and filled in the details of when the group was to start, expected time out and place to visit.

"Okay fellows. Ensure you take only what you need for this

part of the trek," Mike said. "Check your abseil gear, helmets, spare karabiners and prussick loops."

The boys went through their packs and one by one replied they were good to go. Cameron took the lead along the four-wheel drive service track. This part of the track was used by bushfire brigade trucks in time of fires. The sandy track soon gave way to a bush track as it rose high on the peninsula and the surrounding rugged valleys could be seen. The group stopped atop a large rock and took in the view. It was nothing short of magnificent. In front of the group a large valley stood, waiting to be explored. On the opposite side to the group were sheer rock walls that looked like honeycomb sheets. The scenery was unspoilt. It would not have looked out of place to see large dinosaurs roaming around.

Scott took in the view with some trepidation. "So, we have to climb out this high after being all the way down there?"

Mike was about to answer when Cameron replied.

"Each one of you is pretty fit, so we shouldn't have too much of a problem getting out. It will just be a long day for all of us."

"How do we actually get off the valley floor? Is there a trail like this that is easy to walk out?"

"No and yes. The track in, is the track out, almost. When we clear the last abseil, we have a large rock face to climb without ropes. It is about a 60-degree slope but has some great views on the top.

"Once we clear this part there is a walking track for a little while then we have to walk up a small rock face before rejoining the bush track, we're on now."

Mike said they would complete a circular route, but the adventure would be worth it. Cameron started heading off again after the photo session of the group with the valley backdrop. A short way from the rock outcrop the group started descending into the valley.

"Notice the cairn near the bush line," Mike said.

"We go to the left now and will walk back to here from the right."

"What's a cairn?" Mark asked.

Mike bent down near the pile of rocks and pointed to it. The rock pile was only half a metre high and started with a large flat rock and a series of smaller ones on top of each other.

"If ever you get into trouble in the bush and want to leave a message, you normally build a cairn on the track and place your message inside with a handkerchief or some other cloth hanging out," Cameron said.

"Alright, I'll bite," Scott said.

"Why place the hanky in the cairn?"

"That's so rescuers' attention will be drawn to the cairn and also the cloth lasts longer than paper in adverse conditions."

The team moved on and started climbing down a gentle slope as rock walls started to raise either side of them. The group was still high compared to the valley below them.

"This is looking ominous," Peter said to Mark.

"I'll say. I'm looking forward to the canyons but not the walk out.

"I'm with you."

Scott pointed to the rock walls and looked directly at Brett. "Yeah, I don't like the way the walls are coming together …

It looks like a giant river must have flown through here eons ago."

"Well, we know that's how all this was formed … but hell, what a river it must have been!"

The boys stopped in their tracks. Ahead of them was a small glen where the rock walls almost met. A large tree guarded a huge horizontal slit in the rock walls that had semi-circular depressions like rock pools.

"This is our first abseil," Mike said. "We have to traverse along the slit and then chimney down to the chamber below. After that, we do a small abseil to get further down into the chamber, walk through knee-high water and out onto a path."

Easier said than done, Scott thought. He watched nervously as Cameron walked along the rock face with his legs wide open and keeping his balance. Cameron moved to one side of the open slit, sat down and peered through the opening.

"Mike it's not too wet down the slopes so we should be okay," Cameron said.

"I suggest we set up an emergency line around the tree at the entrance and if needed, anyone can put a prussick loop around the line and onto their abseil harness."

"Thanks Cameron. Mark and Ian grab the medium sized rope and put it through the metal shackle that's around the tree, please. Ensure the rope is at the half-way point on the shackle and …"

"Tie figure eight knots on each of the two ends," Ian said with a smile as he started lifting the rope.

Commercial adventure companies used the route the Venturers were taking and left small safety lines with shackle bolts through them, around the obvious abseil points and entry to the various canyons. This made it easier for Mike and his Unit but still had to be checked to ensure they were safe before they were used. Scott watched Cameron slowly inch his way into the canyon. The tall Rover had to lower himself bit by bit into the rocky slit keeping a three-point contact always with his body and the rock wall. Within minutes Cameron was nowhere to be seen.

Mike got the rope that had been fed through the shackle and walked it along the rocky slit. He sat near where Cameron seemed to disappear into the earth and put his feet across the rock opening. Mike then fed the rope over his feet and down into the opening.

"Below!" Mike shouted to Cameron as the rope slowly snaked its way through the slit and down to the Rover waiting below.

"Got it, Mike. It's pretty wet down here, but the rock walls are reasonably dry for the boys to chimney down."

"Okay thanks, mate."

Mike turned to the Venturers and told them about the canyon condition. "Remember, take your time, really push your back against the rock wall and alternate your feet as you drop down. Use your hands for any handhold you can and keep three points of your body on the walls at all times until you are down."

Mark was first to make his way from the glen to the rocky slit. He was the smallest Venturer but was probably the most agile. Mark walked along the rocky slit and around Mike. He sat down in the circular opening area where Cameron had gone and gave Mike the thumbs up. Mike asked him whether he wanted to self-belay himself by prussicking down the rope. Mark gave a nervous smile and declined. He started shuffling his body down through the opening and along the opposing rock walls.

"That's it, Mark. There's a handhold to your left ... just down a bit. Now move your right leg down to the next little bump," Cameron said as he directed Mark down the walls.

Mike sat passively watching Mark's helmet slowly work its way down the rock walls to the rock pools below. Mark looked up, put his thumb up into the air to Mike and yelled 'Next'.

Scott took a deep breath as he made his way from the nice grassy glen out along the rock slit to Mike. He hadn't done much chimneying before and was nervous. Scott decided he would not tie a prussick loop around the abseil rope as it would be more hindrance than help. He walked around Mike and sat in the circular opening and straddled the slit. It took a few moments before he could make out Cameron and Mark as they were enveloped in shadows.

Slowly Scott inched his way down into the opening – stretching his legs out in front of him and pushing his backpack into the opposite wall. A number of times he asked himself why he was doing this. A good abseil yes. An easy to reasonable rock climb yes. But climbing down an opening between two rock walls seemed ludicrous.

"Reach more to your left Scott," Cameron said.

"There's also a better foothold just down a little further ... keep going. That's it."

Scott was glad Cameron had come along and was the

first down the slot. Cameron was the older brother you never had. He was great with all the Venturers. Cameron cared for everyone. He had also been instrumental in backing Scott's idea for a Rover Rescue Service and had started his training with a Police Rescue Unit.

Scott started to falter and slip as he lost his footing along the wall in front of him. He tried to push his back into the rear wall and hold on to the wall in front but slid uncontrollably. Cameron saw Scott's expression of panic and quickly scrambled up the side of one of the walls. He never yelled out in case it panicked the boy but just formed a human arch between the two walls for Scott to land. Scott's backpack kept sliding as the Venturer lost his balance altogether and he landed on Cameron's back in a sitting position.

"Are you okay, Scott?" Cameron asked.

Scott grabbed the rock wall in front of him and held on. He was safe, just grazed around the hands and arms.

"Thanks Cameron. My feet weren't strong enough to straddle the little column and take my weight as I arched back," Scott said.

"Next time tie on your prussick loop as it would have stopped you from falling too far. Remember – better to be safe than sorry."

"No probs. Sorry if I hurt you."

"No. I'm fine."

Scott slowly climbed off Cameron and down the rocky slope and into the icy cold knee-high water. He washed his hands and face and followed the river course forward until he found Mark who was sitting on a dry rock near the abseil point.

"What happened? Did you fall?" Mark asked.

"I lost my footing and couldn't regain a handhold. Lucky for me, Cameron saw me going and formed a human mattress for me to fall onto."

"Yes. He's good like that. How come you didn't use a prussick loop? It would have broken your fall."

"I thought it would actually get in my way and make it harder for me to descend. I'll know better next time."

Cameron dusted himself off and told Mike what had happened. He suggested the rest of the Venturers all have prussick loops on to save any problems. Mike relayed Cameron's conversation with him and ensured each of the other Venturers tied their prussick loops around the rope before descending down into the canyon.

The other Venturers made it to the bottom without incident – even the Unit Chairman, Peter, who was awkward at the best of times. After the final youth had said he was down, Mike started his descent. He had done lots of chimneying before and was almost graceful in his movements. Methodically he pushed against the rear wall with his backpack and looked for handholds and places to put his toes and feet on the wall opposite. Slowly he made it to the bottom and into the water.

"Yoiks, I forgot how cold this water is," Mike said to Cameron.

"Yeah, regardless of time of year, this place is always cold. The boys are sitting on rocks around the corner waiting for us."

"Great. I'll start pulling in the rope and looping it together if you want to get them organised for our first little abseil."

"No probs."

Cameron jumped back into the water and walked round the corner of the water chamber. Light streamed in from above but because of the odd shapes of the rock wall, was well filtered. The walls seemed dark at the top because trying to see them against the penetrating light made them so devoid of colour. At the bottom, they were more a sandstone and mud colour.

The Venturers were all talking about their prowess of their first bit of adventure and what it was like for them as they made their way down between the walls. Cameron caught up with them and got them moving again. He pulled off his rucksack and took out a small rope which he gave to Scott to tie off around a set of logs wedged across an opening into a lower water course chamber. Again, professional canyoners had left prussick loops with a metal shackle around them as an abseil anchor point.

Scott and Ian both checked the shackle and prussick loop left around the logs. They then looped their rope through the shackle and ensured each end had a figure of eight knot to stop anyone from abseiling past the ends. Both boys didn't want anyone slipping off the end of the rope. Not in this valley. Rescue would be nigh impossible. The first abseil was only around five metres but it was down a very wet and slippery slope the boys could not have climbed down without injury or a rope. Mike joined the Venturers and Cameron after re-coiling the first rope and stowing it back into his backpack. One by one the Venturers abseiled confidently down the narrow slippery slope and into the final pool of the chamber. The boys each took turns in belaying the next person down before moving out of the canyon and into the open grassed area. Cameron was last this time and pulled the rope down behind him. After coiling his rope and stowing it in his backpack, he joined the group.

"Mike, I think we have a problem brewing," Cameron said quietly.

"The weather's changing pretty fast and looks like it's going to bucket down soon."

"The forecast was for overcast with winds but not storms."

"I'd say a pressure change has happened and we're going to be in the middle of it. We better get a move on as the last abseil and walk out will be hard enough without rain."

"Okay, Cameron. Let's get the boys moving."

Chapter Four

Rain started spitting as the Venturers made their way through another glen. The trees here were enormous and their exposed roots were like giant twisted ropes reaching from the underground to the tree trunks. Take a walk down any maritime quay and you would see the giant ropes used to tie up ships alongside their berths. These roots were similar, it was eerie. The area was almost sub-tropical with its large ferns and mossy patches. The temperature was a cooler five to 10 degrees than that in the open valley.

The rock wall on the left was smooth and a light yellow and amber in colour like honeycomb where the wind had eroded its rough features. On the right, the rock wall was rough and dark like chocolate dipped with rice bubbles. It would have been easy to imagine movies about prehistoric times being shot here. The Venturers made their way along a creek line that stretched between the two rock walls until they came to a rocky overhang that seemed to lead down to the valley floor.

Initially, the sight of the height of the overhang compared to the valley walls a few kilometres away spooked the boys. They thought they would be abseiling down the equivalent of a 30-storey building. Trees on the valley top were starting to sway as a cold wind began to blow. Spots of rain soon turned to continuous sheets of rain forcing the boys to dive into their back packs to retrieve their raincoats. Cameron moved forward to the edge of the overhang. A large gum tree stood anchored a metre from the edge and had two prussick loops and a metal shackle tied to its base.

Cameron got Brett to take out the large rope, tie himself onto the prussick loops and thread the rope through the shackle. Brett worked hard to uncoil the rope in the pouring rain and put the middle through the shackle. He was about to throw the rope over the edge when he looked up at Scott who was pointing to the rope ends. A smile broke out across Brett's face, and he tied figure of eight knots around each of the standing ends.

"Okay Cameron will go first and belay the next person," Mike said.

"This jump is only around 17 metres. At the bottom are a track that winds around the rock walls down to the final canyon and the track out.

"Watch the tree on your right on the way down. It grew from between two rocks that form this overhang … pretty strange."

Cameron threaded his abseiling device with the rope, tied off and then undid his prussick loop to the shackle.

"See you downstairs."

Mike was standing near the tree and had tied his prussick loop around the tree. He called Ian to be next and then went through the routine of tying him onto a prussick loop, getting him to put himself on the abseil, tie off the rope and then undo the prussick loop. After untying the main rope from his abseil gear, Ian was ready to abseil. Mike repeated the same procedure with each of the boys as their turns came up leaving Brett and Scott to go last. The wind picked up quite heavily and lightning started to flash across the length of the valley. The rain was continuous and the drop in temperature made small clouds of steam emanate from each of the boys as they breathed.

"Mike! Mike!" Cameron yelled from the bottom of the abseil.

Mike leant over the edge of the cliff where he could view Cameron better.

"What's up?"

"Be careful of the ledge on your left as there is a large bird's nest with a couple of eggs in it."

Mike crouched to his knees and then lay on his stomach to peer over the ledge more fully. He saw the nest and started to scan the sky for the eggs' parents. He pulled himself up and spoke to Brett and Scott.

"Okay guys be careful of the nest on the ledge below otherwise we could have some bird problems we don't need."

Brett hooked up to the prussick loop and tied himself onto the abseiling rope. He checked his gear and then asked Mike to double check he was right to abseil. Mike held the shoulder of Brett as he strained to hear what he thought was someone calling. He looked down at Cameron and the other Venturers below, but they were talking among themselves. Brett unhooked his prussick loop and started to edge back on the cliff. He took two small steps down when two shadows crossed over him.

A loud cacophony of screeching suddenly echoed

throughout the valley. Mike looked up and saw two peregrine falcons flying above the cliff in an upward arc. He yelled to Brett to be careful. However, the screeching increased in intensity and the constant '*kee, kee, kee, kee*' emanating from the falcons intensified. The bigger of the two birds led the way and swooped towards Brett's head. The youth used his left hand to try and brush the bird away while maintaining a grip on the abseil rope from behind with his right hand. It happened so fast and without warning. While Brett was brushing the first falcon away the second darted towards the youth. Instinctively, Brett pushed out from the cliff face and tried to brush the falcons away with both hands as he was worried they would attack his head or eyes. Mike and Scott watched in horror as Brett pushed hard away from the cliff with both his arms flailing in the air. Instead of falling in a line down the cliff where Ian was belaying, he landed on a small branch in a gum tree a metre down.

Brett's face was contorted as he writhed in agony and began his own screeching of pain. He had landed halfway along the branch on his back and could not move. A small branch had pierced his back and the boy was stuck fast. Ian went to pull the rope tight to prevent Brett falling but Cameron stopped him. Mike and Scott looked on in shock as blood started to seep between Brett and the branch and start dripping down to the Venturers below. Mike yelled across to Brett not to move and to stay calm. He looked carefully at the branch holding his Venturer and determined his own added weight could break the bough and send both he and Brett into a disastrous fall. Scott had tears in his eyes as he helplessly watched his best friend writhe in pain. He too was worried the back piercing could be a fatal blow to Brett.

Cameron and the Venturers below were becoming agitated by the dripping blood and the fact Mike had made no move towards Brett.

"Cameron, I can't get to him. The branch won't hold both our weights," Mike said.

"Brett doesn't seem to be able to do much either."

"What about Scott? Can he use the second rope and abseil into the tree and work on Brett?"

Scott looked at Mike and swallowed hard. What Cameron was asking didn't seem hard. It was just a very dangerous way of abseiling. The thought of not trying to help his friend and later finding out Brett had died because of his inaction made Scott dry retch. Mike kept trying to talk to Brett and simultaneously calm Scott. There was a chance Scott could abseil into the tree, position himself on the branch near the main trunk and tie himself off. Scott would have to work to tie onto Brett so he couldn't fall any further and then try and deal with his back injury. This was a moment for paramount courage.

"Scott, do you think you could abseil into the tree and help Brett?" Mike asked.

Scott was trembling and wiped the tears from his eyes. He looked his Venturer Leader in the eyes and said he knew Brett would do it for him.

"Okay, this is going to be a hard and messy operation, but I'll stay with you all the way.

"The first thing we'll do is get the second rope I have and

tie it around the prussick loop. This way, you'll be attached all the time.

"You'll have to tie your own prussick loop on the abseil rope and self-belay as this rope won't reach the bottom of the cliff. It will reach into the tree where you can tie off.

"You'll then have to tie Brett to you as well and give me a report on his wound. Whatever happens, no matter how this turns out, I need you to stay calm and fully alert – like you were with the Russian mobsters at our Christmas camp all those eons ago."

"Mike, I can do it. I've got my first aid kit and my raincoat to keep warm. My camelback is quite full, so I've got plenty of water."

Rain started falling heavily and Scott found it hard to tell whether Mike had tears in his eyes or his face was just wet from the rain. Mike looked down to Cameron and said he would have to take the Venturers out and back to the cars before the rivers became swollen and flash flooding stopped them climbing out to safety.

Cameron started arguing and then stopped. He saw the look on the faces of the Venturers around him and knew he had to save their lives before they too became in peril. It was an awkward safety situation. Cameron could have stayed to try and help Mike and Scott as they battled to lower Brett down. The argument was lost when he counted the six boys in front of him.

Mike's rope was not long enough to reach the bottom of the cliff. Brett had the abseil rope around him and caught in the bough of the tree. Cameron did not have any rock-climbing equipment to effect a rescue from the bottom of the cliff and his bouldering skills were of no use here.

"We'll wait to see how Scott goes," Cameron said.

"Then we'll assess the situation from there."

"Okay." Mike said.

Mike put his hands on Scott's shoulders and said this next part was up to him. He told him he had the skills to do the task. He just needed an inner voice to tell him he could do it.

"I hear you and the voice," Scott said.

"However, if those bloody falcons come anywhere near Brett or me, I'll freak."

"Don't worry. Now I know the falcons are in the area, I'll keep a look out. I'll throw sticks at them if they come anywhere near you."

"Okay."

The rain pelted down and thunder rolled across the valley as a distant '*kee, kee, kee, kee*' could be heard. Scott tied himself onto the prussick loop and then tied himself onto the second abseil rope. He looked to where Brett lay motionless on the branch with a black, maroon stain around his T-shirt and bright red drip marks leading down the branch. Scott undid the prussick loop and prepared himself. Mike spoke calmly and reassuringly to him.

"Think back to the Russians, Scott. You overcame your fears and saved us all. Now, you have to save Brett. We'll talk through what to do with Brett once you have assessed him and let me know. Okay?"

"Okay, boss."

Scott stepped down one pace and stopped. He looked at

Brett and gauged where he would land once he pushed himself from the cliff. The high screeching '*kee, kee, kee, kee*' could be heard in the distance. Mike had a large stick in his hands and readied himself to ward off the falcons if they came to attack Scott. Rain continued falling heavily and formed an aqua curtain across the valley shielding onlookers from what was happening on the other side of the open space between the massive rock walls. Scott stepped down one more pace and looked up. He saw Mike moving his big stick in the air. He looked across to the bough and mechanically worked out the amount of effort needed to get into the tree.

The youth virtually squatted on his ankles and with one large effort pushed out from the cliff to abseil to the tree. Scott reached out and grabbed the branch where Brett was lying and held tight. He scrambled onto the fork of the branch and the main trunk. Slowly, the gangly youth made his way into the fork and sat up straddling the branch. He reached down to his prussick loop and adjusted it before locking off his abseiling gear. If he fell, he would only fall a short way before his prussick held tight. Scott pulled up the trailing part of the rope and tied it off around the tree trunk. Now he couldn't fall.

He tried to talk to Brett but initially couldn't get his voice to work. He was emotional. Bit by bit, Scott inched his way along the branch where Brett was draped. He could hear his mate breathing hard and saw Brett was unconscious.

Scott called softly to Brett a couple of times and got no response. He then gingerly crawled closer to Brett along the bough and surveyed why his mate had not fallen any further. Brett was draped over the bough. The branch had pierced his back above his hips and was stuck hard inside Brett. He was impaled.

"Mike, the branch is stuck right inside his back," Scott yelled across to Mike.

"He's still bleeding but is unconscious."

"Okay Scott. If you lift him up more than likely the branch will snap off. If you don't lift him, he's just going to put continuous pressure on the inside of his back and possibly cause more problems.

"Also, if he wakes with a fright he'll fall and could die. I think we have no choice but to tie him to the rope and actually try and sit him up with you in the fork.

"This will be tricky. Whatever happens, you can't pull the branch out from his back or you'll never stop the bleeding."

Scott nodded his head in agreeance. He saw Mike cup his hands and look down at Cameron and the other Venturers.

"Cameron. Brett's too badly injured to try and get him down or out of the canyon," Mike yelled.

"We'll try and stabilise him here in the tree. You'll have to get the boys out before any flash flooding comes.

"Ring the emergency services and …"

"Don't forget to ring the *1 900-scout* number as this has started to be manned now," Scott broke in.

Cameron knew he had no choice but leave Mike and Scott to deal with Brett so he could get the other boys out safely. This would be a trip no one would forget. The trick for Cameron now was to get through the last canyon and climb out quickly. Before any flash flooding stopped their exit and swept them away downstream. For Scott and Mike, it was to stabilise Brett and wait for help while shooing away any peregrine falcons that may return to the site. The Venturers on the ground were angry they couldn't help Scott and Mike but understood they had to get to safety too or their lives would be claimed.

Cameron and the Venturers yelled out to Scott and Mike amid loud rolling thunder and started on their way out. Scott grabbed the rope he was on and started to feed it under and around Brett. His hands became sticky with Brett's blood as he wound the rope around his mate and tied him off. He kept talking to Brett in a calm low voice in case his mate moved or woke up. This was not going to be easy. Scott inched forward onto Brett's legs and reached under his mate's arm pit. He tried to raise him to a sitting position but found the branch impaling Brett was stopping any forward movement.

"Are you able to snap the branch in Brett's back near its base," Mike asked. "It would make it easier for you."

"I'll try but it is quite awkward."

Scott tried lifting Brett forward again and then felt for the branch in his back. It was around the size of a half-closed fist and had little give. He reached into his left pants pocket and took out his handkerchief. The nicely ironed cloth was unfolded. Scott then brought Brett's hands together and tied them up. Scott inched a bit further forward along Brett and placed his mate's hands over his head. Brett looked like a wounded Prisoner of War with his hands tied and blood still oozing from his back. With a concerted effort Scott raised Brett forward again. The branch in Brett's back became more exposed and Scott reached around Brett with both hands. He grabbed the branch in a tight stranglehold and then exerted pressure from both hands in an opposite direction.

At first the branch wouldn't give. Scott called on every bit of inner strength he had, closed his eyes and in a feat of super strength, broke the branch from its mainstream trunk. Scott had called on the same strength people in major accidents call on to help achieve the near impossible. After all, this was his best friend who seemed to be dying in front of him. Scott lurched backwards with Brett draped over his shoulders like a heavy doll. He inched his way back to the main fork in the tree with his mate straddled around the same branch. Now, to fix Brett's wound and untie his mate.

"Well done, Scott," Mike yelled.

He had watched his young charge go through the paces of trying to help his mate in extraordinary circumstances and then work out what best way to do it. Amazed, Mike watched Scott close his eyes and summon every bit of strength, he had to break the branch and free Brett. He had bitten his tongue in wanting to call out from his cliff top point across top the gum tree to tell Scott what to do. Instead, the youth had instinctively known what to do and just did it. Mike looked on with total admiration and joy for Scott as he saw the youth move backwards to the tree trunk with Brett draped over him.

"Now you'll have to fix his wound and keep him draped over you until rescue arrives. Can you handle it?"

"Yeah, I don't know where I found the strength to break the branch, but I did. I guess I was so angry at the birds who caused this, and the injuries Brett has received I just snapped the branch."

"Mate, I'm very proud of you. The other boys and Cameron would be proud of you. More importantly, Brett will too, when this is all over."

Scott reached into his first aid 'bum pack', what the Americans would call a 'fanny bag' and took out a thick cloth pad. He fashioned it into a circle and reached under Brett's T-shirt at the back. Scott placed the round pad over the branch piece sticking out of Brett's back. He then reached back into his first aid bag and pulled out a sling. Slowly, he manoeuvred it under Brett's T-shirt and around his torso above the circular pad. Scott tied off the sling on Brett's side as tight as he could. He then felt Brett's back where his wound was to see if the bleeding had stopped. It had.

Relief washed over Scott as he leaned back into the trunk with Brett draped over him. He was exhausted and tired. Now he had stemmed the bleeding and put Brett into a safer position he was happy. Scott tried to relax. He was sitting on a fork of a tree with his best mate draped over him and tied to the trunk. The floor of the valley was around 17 metres below – enough to kill both Brett and him if they fell.

At the cliff top stood Mike with a large stick in hand. The rain pelted down and the valley became an echo point for the thunder and lightning. Scott cuddled Brett and kept talking softly in his ear as to what had been happening. He drew a large breath and began to relax. This could be a long wait for rescue. A thought ran through Scott's mind, and he pulled out his mobile phone. He tried to call the *1 900-scout* number but failed to connect. Scott pulled the phone from his face and tried the number again. He watched as the GPRS signal wavered.

This told him some signal could get out but was dependent on weather conditions.

Scott held the phone in his hand and thought about it. He remembered the emergency 112 number for his mobile phone and tried that. The signal also wavered on and off. Scott thought for a moment and went looking through his phone's directory. He found what he wanted. In the Australian system dialling 106 on a mobile phone allows text to be sent to a emergency call centre number for people with hearing or speech impairment. The youth got busy as he started to text what had happened and where. He told of Brett's condition and the worsening weather conditions. There was no reply. Scott sent the message again and then put the phone in his chest pocket.

He kept talking to Brett and feeling around his mate's back to ensure the bleeding had stopped. Brett was still unconscious and was breathing heavy. Each of his breaths was laboured. Scott kept talking to him.

"Scott, stroke Brett's face as you talk to him," Mike yelled.

"Sometimes those unconscious hear what you are saying but just can't respond. The touch will add the extra reassurance. Cameron should be out of the valley and to a point where he can contact the Police in a few hours. We can make it. Hang in there."

Scott started stroking Brett's face and telling him what was happening. All was well as they sat stuck in a tree 17 metres off the ground with a branch end stuck in Brett's back. Mike sat tied to a tree at the edge of the cliff with a large stick by his side – ready to ward off any falcon that wanted to fly in and attack either he or the boys.

Chapter Five

Cameron did something he had never done before. He tried to rush the boys off the valley floor and up the first climb in record time. They were young, fit and driven by an emergency. The adrenalin push would be very high.

Water had started gushing down the creek bed as the boys had made their way to the last canyon. Danger was rife as water poured down the normally dry hole the boys had to descend through the earth. Cameron had marshalled Peter, Ian, Mark, and the rest of the boys around a track on the upward slope of the southern side of a cliff face. They saw the familiar prussick loop with metal device around a tree and were comforted they were on the right track out. Their problem was to beat the river flow before it hit their area from the rain deluge further upstream.

"See that tiny triangular hole over there," Cameron said to the boys.

"That's our entry point. This one is doubly hard. Ordinarily you must chivvy down the hole and into the chamber below. However, this rain has made it very hard with the amount of water pouring in to the hole as well and making the whole space so slippery. I have confidence in each of you as Mike has, that you can do it. Remember, we are in a hurry to get to an area to telephone in but also, we must be extra cautious as we make our way down this last chamber.

"Are you up for it?"

The boys looked at each other and raised their right fists in unison as they said "Yes," loudly and strongly.

Ian was the first to hook onto the prussick loop and then the abseil rope. The slope down to the hole was easy going. The youth stopped as he tried to sit astride the hole and lower himself into the opening. Water was starting to gush around him as he pushed against the back wall. Slowly he lowered himself. His left hand was grating between the cliff top and the abseil rope because of the cramped conditions. He pulled his left hand away from the rope and let some rope run through his right hand. This freed his body from the hole, and he fell under control through the hole and into the chamber below.

It was like two walls had been pushed apart by a superior force and giant rocks placed like marbles on top of each other to form one of the walls. Water was now streaming down the entrance hole to the chamber below. Cameron was worried the chamber would fill with water too quickly before he could get his Venturers out and up onto the slopes.

"Okay. I'm through," Ian yelled.

He abseiled in a controlled fall around 10 metres between the rock walls to the ground and water below. The water was around knee high and slowly rising as the rain pelted down across the valley. Ian looked up and saw sheets of water pouring through the hole he just descended. He unhooked his self-belay and untied from the abseil rope. He then married the ends of the abseil rope around him and yelled out.

"Ready to belay!"

Cameron started sending the other Venturers down one by one and each in turn took over the belaying of the next one on the rope until he made his entrance into the chamber.

"Yoiks, this is the deepest I have experienced water here," Cameron said. "It's not normally waist high and rising. It's usually just a trickle. Everything's okay. We can still make our exit point from the valley before this stream builds up too high as long as we methodically pace ourselves. Are you still with me?"

A rousing chorus of 'yes' rose up from the Venturers. They were tired, angry, but driven with a mission to save themselves and get help to their injured Venturer.

"I hope Brett and Scott are okay," Peter said. "This will be a long day and night for them."

"They'll be fine. They have Mike with them and he's never let us down," Ian said.

Mark couldn't hold back either. "Those three will be fine as long as we can get our fat behinds out of here and in an area where we can ring for emergency services …"

"We should try the number Scott helped set up," Peter said.

"Yeah, and then the other emergency services as they have the helicopters to get them out," Mark butted in.

Cameron could see the boys getting worried again and wanted to re-focus them on the task ahead.

"All three will be fine; otherwise, I wouldn't have left them. It's now up to us to direct every bit of emergency manpower to our people as soon as possible. We have a special task, and we must carry it out. If this means run up the hill ahead, then so be it. We can do it. We can do it for Brett, Scott, and Mike, come on!"

The boys pulled the abseil rope down and re-coiled it before stowing it in Cameron's backpack. They waded their way through the waist high deep water and out into grey lit day punctuated with heavy rain and rolling thunder. The boys walked through the sub-tropical glen between the mouths of two rock walls. They came to a dead end and looked up.

"Do we have to climb that?" Ian asked in exasperation.

"Yes. I have every confidence you will not only make it but do so in good timings as your mates' lives are on the line in real time," Cameron said.

The boys looked up at the goat track made through the loose earth and rocks above them. The slope was on a 60-degree incline upwards.

There were no prussick loops or emergency rope lines to hold on to. No large trees to anchor safety lines were present. There was just a forbidding climb in mud, loose dirt, and rock, up a tortuous incline.

"The longer we look up, the wetter and more slippery this slope will become," Cameron said.

"We must start negotiating this one quickly before it becomes impassable. Otherwise, the walk around is not only dangerous, as it is through swollen rivers, but more time consuming for Scott and Brett and Mike."

The point was made. Cameron took the lead to show the boys the path up through the loose gravel, rocks and broken tree branches that littered the way. Every step was a pain for each of the boys as they pushed themselves upwards, grabbing any solid rock or bush on the way up to help pull them along. It was a hard hill climb. The boys were soon becoming exhausted. The determination and courage in each of the boys showed through as they pushed themselves up the slope. A couple of times some of them slipped. Each time, the other Venturers would anchor themselves against a rock and block their mate from going past them. It was a team effort.

"You know, Mike has a great way to overcome problems like this," Cameron said between disjointed breaths.

"Help me out will you ..."

Cameron started telling a story about Superman and then stopped with the superhero in a predicament. It was then up to the boys to add to the story to keep it alive with some way for the caped hero to get out of his situation or into another one. Mike always did this in times of trouble or pure exhaustion to help change the mindset of the Venturers who were being challenged physically during outdoor activities.

Peter saw the merit in what Cameron was trying to do and joined in to back his pseudo leader.

The other boys joined in begrudgingly as they slowly stepped, pushed, pulled and trudged their way up the very steep hill that was on about a 60-degree incline from the bottom. This was not their way of passing time, but it did help. It was more scouting specific to them. However, the story telling took their minds off the arduous, slippery climb. Cameron chanced a look behind to see the boys clawing their way up the track in rhythm. He felt good. Mike had trained them well and they worked fantastically as a team.

Ian thought he was fit. He was a forward in his soccer team

and although he officially trained once a week and played on Saturdays, he also played a series of ad hoc games with his neighbours at the local soccer field. Here, he was huffing and puffing as he clawed and pulled his way forward and upward.

"This isn't exactly easy, is it?" he asked Cameron.

"No. But imagine trying to haul, pull and lug Brett up here without further injuring him."

"There's no way he would have made it in one piece ... Even if we got the branch out of his back and he stopped bleeding.

"You're right. The only safe place for him was up that bloody tree where hopefully a helicopter can rescue him."

The other boys agreed, grunted, sighed and kept pushing upwards.

"Jeez, I'm going to be sore tomorrow," Mark said as he hauled himself up and over a large rock. "Actually ... look out below," he yelled mid-sentence as he put his weight on a rock dislodging it and sending in tumbling down towards Peter.

The Unit Chairman looked up in surprise and dived to the side in time for the rock to pass. He wasn't annoyed, as it had happened several times to the whole of the party on this leg of the journey out. Twice, Cameron called a stop while his party rested. They were able to look across the valley between the wind squalls and rain. Lightning provided a wonderful light show as it lit up each of the various fingers of the valleys – the high cliff walls forming the respective valley walls.

"How come you took us canyoning in this weather?" Ian asked Cameron as he raised his right hand and pointed to the rain and lightning.

"When Mike and I set today's date we checked and double checked the weather patterns," Cameron replied.

"The last forecast had today as overcast with variable winds but no rain. I don't think even the weather bureau foresaw this storm hitting here before we set out. Think about it. There's no way Mike would place you in danger ... Especially where something like what has happened to Brett has taken place."

The boys agreed and stood up to move on. They had a mission to complete, and their fellow Venturer's life was hanging in the balance.

Scott's text messages had been received in the national capital's emergency rescue centre manned by Rovers. Christian Rowe had been monitoring the various electronic maps of the states on the main operations wall when Scott's text messages were received. Steven Goletz was half-way through his second coffee of the day when his satellite computer started to buzz with Scott's messages.

"Christian, I think you better look at this. We have a problem, Houston."

Christian checked Steven's computer and swallowed.

"If this is for real, we have a major rescue in the making and we need to get cracking as soon as practicable. This is one person we have to pull all stops out to help. You better start with checking on the Blue Mountains Rover Crews and their ability to crank up a rescue mission. Also check with the Police Rescue and their availability to use a helicopter to get into the Alexander area.

"I'll check with Scott's family to confirm it was his mobile number and get onto the weather bureau."

Allan Morrow was quick to answer the phone.

He had been worried about Scott and his canyoning trip from the beginning. No problem about his training, but about the changing weather patterns.

"Hello, this is Allan."

"Mr Morrow, this is Christian Rowe from the national emergency call centre in Canberra. I need to talk to you about Scott."

Allan's heart sank. This was the call he was dreading. Once Christian Rowe had checked the bona fides of Scott's mobile phone number and other details with his father he swung into action. Rover Crews throughout the Blue Mountains region and either side were notified of the incident and Scott's predicament. Calls to Rovers to report to their Crew headquarters and prepare to move to Alexander went out. Text and voice messages burned the airwaves about Scott as the call for help picked up like a rising flood tide.

Crews across Sydney were being told of the problem and the race to try and help Scott and Brett began in earnest. Scott had made a major impression with Venturers and Rovers the year before when he helped rescue his Venturers from a group of Russian drug mafia. The story went international and set Scott up as a national hero. When he was nominated as the driving force behind the Rover led national emergency centre for scouts, Scott became a very wanted person by Crews who vied for him to be a member. A Rover who knew Scott and his family and heard about the call to help was working at a national radio station. He told his news producer of the rescue attempt underway and the story was quickly picked up.

Within minutes, the story of Scott being stuck in a tree in the wild Blue Mountains, trying to save Brett was being flashed around the country. TV stations picked up on the news reports and started running newsflash banners across their programs. The Blue Mountains Police Rescue Squad and its auxiliary Rover Rescue Service were called on to assist with the rescue. The helicopter rescue service was inoperative because of the high winds and foul weather.

The scout emergency hotline was inundated with offers of help and a real coordination role was put into place to sort out rescue efforts. Extra staff was pressed into service to handle the volume of calls as the national Rover phone network swung into action. Media helicopters were not allowed to fly to the Alexander valley area because of the high winds and continuous lightning. Rover crews trained in rescue procedures started driving to Mt Elizabeth in the Blue Mountains where a makeshift emergency centre was being set up. Ambulance paramedics trained in mountain rescue procedures were called to assist. A race had begun between the Police and Rovers to reach Scott, Brett, and Mike. The Rovers wanted to be seen to be effective and to have the chance to rescue their own organisation's people. The Police were keen to show they themselves, were the best trained to handle the situation. The Police set up a series of roadblocks on the roads leading to the Zig Zag railway to prevent unwanted traffic on the roads.

Allan Morrow had started cranking up his own support. He knew a lot of Police who were sympathetic to scouts – especially after Scott's Christmas adventure with the Russian mafia.

He was keen to go to the Blue Mountains and join in the search for Scott but wanted to be at home to support his wife, Kelly. Allan was no fool. He would leave the rescue to the experts. His expertise was the Highway Patrol. Allan went to the fridge in his kitchen and checked the list of Venturers and their contact details Scott had left there with magnetic holders. He found Brett's contacts and rang his father, Rod. The two men chatted for some time and Allan organised for Rod and his wife Leonie to be taken by Highway Patrol to the Blue Mountains to be near the search operations centre for when the boys were retrieved. It was a time to close ranks again and ensure anyone who could help the boys was in play.

Prime Minister Robert Anthony was handed a note during a trade briefing he was conducting in Sydney. He paused, took off his glasses and asked his aide what was needed. The aide told him all civil and police helicopters had been grounded in the area because of the storms. The only ones who trained in these conditions were the Commandos. The Prime Minister paused and reflected. He knew the background to Scott's dramatic rescue of his Venturers when they tangled with the Russian mafia last year. He was quick to lend political support to Scott's idea of the Rover Emergency Rescue Crews. Now the boy himself, and his mate, needed help. It was ironic but again, Robert Anthony had the power to assist someone who was shaping to be a national hero.

"Check to see the Chief of the Defence Force is happy offering a crew from the Commandos and their Blackhawk to go and assist," the Prime Minister said. "This boy deserves every support we can give him. He has my full support."

Mr Anthony then continued his discussions with the American delegation. Back-channel calls were made from the Chief of Defence's office to the New South Wales Police Minister Grant Delaney advising Defence would be amenable to assisting Police if requested. The weather worsened and major storms kept rolling into the valleys surrounding the plateau leading to where Mike and Cameron had parked their cars. At Holsworthy, south of Sydney, the Army's Aviation Squadron's detachment of Blackhawk helicopters sat in hangars. The helicopters were used with the Commandos who conducted special operations duties including anti-terrorism training.

Sergeant Paul Pickering was a career soldier and had served in East Timor, Iraq, and Afghanistan. He had been watching the news when he heard about Scott's plight. He called his second-in-charge Corporal David Parish to his office.

"Mate, what was the name of the Venturer Unit we took abseiling on our training wall earlier this year?"

"Why? Are they in some sort of trouble?"

"Yes. But not Police trouble," Pickering replied.

"They were from 1st Hurstville, I think. You remember that kid Scott was involved in Operation Stella where we chased the Russian mother ship."

"Well, he's in need of help again. He's stuck in a tree with an injured Venturer friend up at Alexander. The Police can't fly in as the weather up there has grounded their birds."

"You know Sarge, we've been waiting for foul weather to conduct some prepatory black ops training. This could be just what we need."

"David we can't just fly in and put our troops at risk, especially without a call from the Police requesting we give them aid."

"Sarge, you're right as usual. I'll check with Police Operations on the backchannel and see whether they are willing to task us?"

"Make the call and I'll talk to the Colonel."

It took a bit of time for the New South Wales Police Minister to see the value of the opportunity laid out for him by Defence and Police. He officially asked Defence to assist his Police in the rescue operations. Virtually all balls were now in play to help Scott, Brett, and Mike. They just needed to hang on and manage the ailing Venturer until help arrived.

Chapter Six

B rett coughed up some blood. He was still unconscious and draped over Scott like a rag doll. The boy's involuntary movement initially gave Scott hope his mate was about to wake. Scott kept talking with Brett, leaned him back and cleaned the blood from his face. Mike had made a temporary shelter from his hutchie or rectangular piece of army vinyl sheeting just back from the cliff ledge. This way he could sit or stand when observing Scott and Brett and be out of most of the rain. His admiration for Scott had increased substantially since the boy had become a Venturer. The youth was always trying to learn, always trying to find solutions to problems. Mike was sure he was going to be an engineer ... if he made it in life to then.

Mike looked at Scott and took in the sight. It would forever be etched into his mind. Rain was still pouring down hard; some lightning could be seen in the far distance. In a tree opposite the cliff ledge sat Scott. He was bestriding a branch with his back to the main tree trunk. Brett was sitting in the opposite direction facing him, with his hands around Scott's shoulders. Scott had placed his raincoat over Brett and had an arm around his mate's back. Every so often Scott would retrieve his hand and check for bleeding from Brett's wound. There was some seepage but no constant bleeding.

Scott retrieved his mobile phone from his chest pocket and saw there were a couple of missed calls. He tried to access the phone when Brett moved and, in the movement, to contain his mate, Scott dropped his phone to the valley floor below where the Venturers and Cameron had stood.

"Mike. Someone tried to ring me. I couldn't see who it was before boofhead here moved and I dropped it."

"Scott, my phone has no network coverage. You must be in a position where the signal just reaches. Problem is that this weather plays havoc with the signals and it is hit and miss until you re-enter the suburbs."

"I hope they got my message."

"Who did you try and send to?"

"I tried to ring the *1 900-scout* number, but it wouldn't connect so I text a couple of messages to the emergency 106 number."

"Good thinking. The emergency text number is part of the emergency 000 telephone number scheme throughout Australia. If they got the message, they'll hopefully act on it. What did you say in your text?"

"I said who I was, where we were, sort of and what had happened to Brett."

"Sounds like you wrote a book."

A cheesy smile came over Scott as he wiped the rain from his face. "No hopefully just enough material to allow someone to catch up with Cameron."

Mike couldn't help himself. "Well done, Scott. I hope it got through. At least we have a fall back with Cameron and the

Venturers. Once they're out it shouldn't take to long for help to be mustered."

Scott lowered his voice and said to him and Brett: "I hope so. I truly hope so."

A huge sigh of relief went up as the last of the Venturers completed the first part of the climb out. They were now exhausted. Cameron was a good task master who kept the morale of the Venturers up as they made their way up the dangerous slope. He knew the climb out was a poor option in the bad weather conditions. The track at the base of the cliff continued for some kilometres and slowly worked its way up through the valley walls.

However, this option would have added quite a few hours to the exit journey. The main consideration was the boys' safety and whether they could actually complete the climb. Cameron had been working with them for a few months in the lead up training for this weekend and saw how they pushed each other. He also saw the tight knit group support one another when anyone got into difficulties. The fitness level of each boy was high also. Lastly, he knew the Venturers would pull out all stops to help Brett in such a dangerous situation.

"Okay do you want to rest or keep going?" Cameron asked.

Peter answered for everyone through gritted teeth.

"We have to push on. We have to get into phone range and get our message out. Come on everyone, push on for Brett. He needs our help."

As one, the Venturers stood on their weary legs and started walking on a more open bush area towards the next tree line point. They were really feeling the pain of the climb and accumulative effect of the walk in, the abseils, chimneying and dreaded climb out.

"What's next?" Mark asked Cameron.

"We have to clear the top of this tree line. It then opens to what canyoners call the Buddhas. These are a series of rounded rock shelves we have to climb before we actually start walking on a formed track."

"Alright, I'll bite. Why are the rocks called the Buddhas?"

"You'll see. The rocks look like a series of little sitting Buddha statues. Once we are on top of these it will be plain sailing back to where our track diverts near the cairn."

The boys started smiling. There was an end to this exhaustive walk coming and it wasn't far away.

"Come on guys, let's pick up our pace," Peter said.

"You have to be kidding, don't you," Ian said as he grimaced with back pain.

"Ian, Brett would be the first to be running for you or anyone else injured. We can do the same for him. Let's go."

"Mr Chairman, you always have a way with words. I'm moving, I'm moving."

Although Cameron was chuffed by the verbal exchange he was also more on his toes in relation to the boys' physical well-being. The last thing he needed now was for one of them to either hurt themselves or suffer from hypothermia.

"Just keep the pace steady and forward and we'll be alright," Cameron said.

In a short time, the group had cleared the tree line and was staring up at the Buddhas. Blue Mountains Rover Crew Leader

Ben Wolfe was secretly glad his Crew had received a call to help out in Scott's rescue. Not that he wished Scott or Brett any harm, far from it. He had been training hard with his Crew members and the State Emergency Services for some time in an effort to bring his Crew up to a good rescue capability. Ordinarily his Crew had a membership of around 15 Rovers, male and female. Today he had been inundated with calls from Rovers both side of the Blue Mountains who wanted to join in the rescue. At last count he and his Crew members had received more than 100 calls from Rovers who said they were packed and on their way to the Blue Mountains. The Rovers saw this as their litmus test in preparation for taking on rescue duties and knew the high Media profile of Scott would attract a lot of Media attention.

Police Sergeant Brian Wallace set up a forward command post in the Mt Elizabeth School of Arts. This was the last suburb and town before the beginning of Coachman's Road and the way into the Alexander Plateau. He too was a veteran, only his wars had been with major rescues of people from overturned vehicles, industrial accidents, and bushwalking mishaps. Once he received a call from the National Emergency Call Centre in Canberra, he took a crew from Katoomba, where he was based and made his way down the mountains to Mt Elizabeth. He had a special rapport with the Local Council and so it was easy to arrange access to the School of Arts building.

He set up a special radio transmitter in the hall along with some extra phone lines. The local State Emergency Service was called on to assist with communications and they set up a large temporary radio transmitter in the rear yard of the premises. Maps of the area around Julia Falls and Thompson Canyon were projected onto the walls of the main room. Police and Rover Crews helped plot the known route in and out of Thompson Canyon by Mike and the Venturers. They also plotted alternative routes the party could take if the rivers became swollen from the rain.

A Rover who was also a Primary School teacher brought an electronic 'Smart Board' along so images could be projected onto it and printouts obtained for ground rescue teams. Ben Wolfe discussed the various options available to rescuers with Sergeant Wallace. The policeman was impressed. Normally by now Police were ready to make their first Media interviews and tell how unprepared the parties that need rescuing were and how only organisations like the Police knew how to handle these situations.

He wasn't disappointed. Within 45 minutes Media outside broadcast vans started arriving at Mt Elizabeth and calls were made for Sergeant Wallace to hold a Media conference. Police Minister Gary Delaney contacted Sergeant Wallace and ordered him not to take the lead in this rescue. He was told to let the Rovers initialise attempts to rescue Scott, Brett and Mike to see if their emergency rescue scheme had been a success. Before he could talk to the Media, Sergeant Wallace received another call. It was Sergeant Pickering from the Commandos. He told his Police counterpart he had been given clearance by the Chief of the Defence Force to attempt a helicopter rescue if it was possible.

Sergeant Wallace was becoming more amazed by the minute. He was receiving continuous reports of Rover Crews with swags of rescue materials, massing along the entrances to the Zig Zag Railway asking if they could help. The very Police roadblocks put in place to stop onlookers was now preventing a growing crowd of Rovers, all keen to help rescue Scott and Brett. At one stage reinforcements of Police were called for because of the swelling numbers of young people in cars waiting to use Coachman's Road and make their way to Thompsons Canyon.

The Rovers were ordered not to drive along Coachman's Road. They didn't. Instead, they parked their cars legally and in tight rows in the public car spaces at either end of the entrances to the Alexander Plateau. They then formed burgeoning groups and started discussing their options and tactics. Sergeant Wallace asked Ben to join him in the first Media conference to explain what had happened and what was being planned. A room to the side of the main part of the School of Arts was set aside for the conference. Ben asked for several Rovers in uniforms to assist. Sergeant Wallace had fronted the Media cameras a few times and was also a professional at this side of the house. However, he held his own counsel as to how Ben should conduct himself. Ben told the waiting crews he would be ready in five minutes. His offsider Stuart Crouch made a call to Canberra. The Media conference was just about to begin when Stuart pulled Ben aside. A huge grin erupted across Ben's face.

"My name is Ben Wolfe and this afternoon we have a major rescue operation in train to retrieve two injured Venturer Scouts and a Venturer Leader from Thompsons Canyon in the Blue Mountains.

"A group of eight Venturers from 1st Hurstville led by their leader Mike Hunter and Rover Cameron Wagstaff went to the canyon early today.

"We believe from early reports they had been properly trained, have correct equipment and have followed all the necessary procedures.

"However, some form of misadventure has taken place that has left two of the boys stuck in a tree with one of the boys impaled on a branch. We believe the party has split when the weather turned foul with Cameron leading the other Venturers out of the valley.

"Their Venturer Leader Mike Hunter has opted to stay with the two boys in the tree."

The Media questions of how the boys became stuck in a tree; why Mike didn't rescue them himself and lead them out and why the boys went canyoning in such dangerous weather started to dog Ben. Sergeant Wallace smiled from the rear of the room. He had seen other Media novices in situations like this. However, his orders were plain and simple. Let the Rovers fall on their own sword. Stuart took the lead.

"I have some breaking news. As you know the heavy rain and lightning in the valleys have prevented rescue and Media helicopters flying in the area. A short time ago the Chief of the Defence Force authorised an Army Blackhawk helicopter to try and rescue the two Venturers in the tree.

"Your Media helicopters can't fly into the valley because of the dangerous air currents and storms. The Blackhawk is one of the best equipped aircraft for the mission. A Blackhawk with a group of Army Commandos will be arriving soon for briefings with the Rovers Crews here and the other emergency services personnel."

The bombshell set the Media into a spin. Several left the room to make their own enquiries and to let their Chiefs of Staff and News directors know the update. It was highly unusual for Defence to get involved in rescue operations. They must be tasked by the State authorities who, for whatever reason, can't do the job themselves. This job had a push from Canberra, the nation's capital and from The Lodge, the Prime Minister's home.

Stuart and Ben did a series of TV and radio interviews. Occasionally Sergeant Wallace was asked to comment, but he tried to stay in the background. Prime Minister Anthony smiled when he saw the news update which mentioned the Rovers national emergency call centre was receiving its baptism of fire with a rescue of two Venturers. He grinned even more when mention was made of the assistance of the Blackhawk helicopter and Commandos. Mr Anthony had ordered his aides to keep him fully informed of developments.

A convoy comprising 10 Rovers with two Police Rescue and two ambulance paramedic members went through the southern roadblock and started making their way along Coachman's Road. They were joined by a convoy of Media vans and vehicles, some with satellite dishes on top. The further the rescue convoy drove along the road, the more Rovers they saw walking along the road with helmets with headlights, as if they were ready to go caving. The Police could not stop the overwhelming numbers of young people who made their way into the bush around the roadblocks. Small groups of Rovers kept linking up with other groups forming a large continuous line of backpacking young men and women, most with large packs full of ropes and other rescue equipment. They were determined to help Scott, Brett, and Mike. This was their time. They were in the spotlight. After all the fanfare about the creation of the Rover Rescue Service and the resultant Media hype, no one wanted this to fail. The additional imperative was to rescue the person who had brought the Rovers to national and international prominence when he needed help.

The Police Rescue members radioed back to the School of Arts operational centre and told them of the huge numbers of Rovers headed towards Thompson Canyon. Two patrol cars were dispatched to the parking area at the end of Coachman's Road where Cameron and Mike had parked their cars. The heavy winds had not abated and the rain was still continuously pelting down in huge squalls. No one seemed to care about the weather except the Commandos and Blackhawk helicopter crew who had been dispatched to the area. Media helicopters were forced to land and wait at Mt Elizabeth until they had official sanction to fly into the valley.

Chapter Seven

Cameron's mind had been racing. He wanted to push the Venturers so hard and so fast so he could get out of the valley quickly and contact authorities. Reality held him back. He had started coming into his adult strength and had a good mental connection between mind and body. Cameron remembered at the boys age, there was a disconnect. These Venturers were trying their hardest. They were keen, but not quite ready for a full-on super push. The tree line was behind them, and the Buddhas became less imposing with every step. The rock wall was a conglomeration of small ledges with a series of large and small rocks that melded into a wall. From a distance the large and small rocks looked like small Buddha statues all sitting in rows.

"Eeha!" Cameron yelled out when the Buddhas were directly in front of them. "Once we are on top of those little babies there is a small track that leads onto a four-wheel drive track and our cars."

"We are very close now."

Ian stopped and looked at the valley below through the continuous sheets of rain. He cupped his hands and gave out a long call. 'Cooeeee.'

The noise resonated across the darkening valley. Within seconds the echo resounded and died down. The boys laughed and continued their climb up the rock wall.

A second 'Cooeeee' emanated from a different direction. Was it Scott and Brett? The boys stopped dead in their tracks. This was not Ian's echo. It was someone else. Ian stopped again, regained his breath, and cupped his hands. With the strongest breath he could muster he yelled out once more.

'Cooeeee.'

Suddenly the valley became alive as a series of 'cooeeees' echoed from atop the valley in front of them.

"It seems to be coming from the same direction where we should find our cars," Cameron said. "It could be anyone. No one knows we have problems yet. I checked my mobile phone a little while ago and there is still no coverage.

"Are you up for a run? The track starts just over the other side of these little rocks."

The Venturers stopped and looked at each other. They were tired, wet, hungry, and exhausted. They had never felt so drained of energy. Something had kicked in to give each of the boys a drive to finish, no matter the cost to them. They were at the summit of the Buddhas and looked across the valley to the walls of the opposing rock faces to the far valleys.

"I'm up for it," Mark said.

"How about it Mr Chairman? Can you muster one last bit of energy to get to the cars?"

"Yes. Ordinarily I would tell you what you could do with yourself ... but not now," Peter said.

"We must get out so we can get help for Brett. We can't let him down, not now. Come on, let's have one last push."

Cameron was moved emotionally. He had never seen such a strong bond of mateship before and was very proud to be part of this moment in time. Ian picked up the pace and the others followed. Within a short time, they stopped again.

"What the hell is that?" Mark asked.

"It sounds like a jamboree or something."

Sounds of people singing were starting to waft through the valleys. The voices were mostly male. Not drunken but energetic.

"*I have that BP feeling, deep in my heart, deep in my...*" kept wafting through the treetops and around the edges of the valley. Cameron started smiling and then laughing.

"There's a lot of Rovers nearby. What we hear is one of their main songs," he said.

"They're letting us know they are nearby. Something has happened. Maybe Scott or Mike got a message out before the storms took hold."

The pace quickened. Cameron started it first and then the boys picked it up.

"*Cooee. Cooee. Cooee...*"

The boys yelled louder and louder. The response was quick and firm.

"*Cooee. Cooee. Cooee...*"

The sounds of the Rovers increased and came from the final tree line leading up to the cars. The forest was alive. Lights moved everywhere.

At first the yellow and white lights were the size of pinheads.

They gradually grew larger and larger like fireflies transforming into locomotive lights with large beams. Cameron and the Venturers started to sprint towards the lights.

"Here they come. Someone get down there with a torch and find out what's going on," a voice yelled.

Within seconds, torches and lights were making their way down the track to Cameron and the Venturers.

"There they are. They're running out."

Iridescent banded jackets and helmets started to come into focus as a large body of people moved down the track from the cars to catch up with Cameron and the Venturers.

"Hi, who are you?" Michael Carter asked as he ran his helmet light up and down Cameron's body and then across to the Venturers as they caught up.

"G'day, I'm Cameron Wagstaff and these are Venturers from 1st Hurstville," an exhausted Cameron said. "There's a Venturer impaled in a tree down at the second abseil at Thompson's Canyon and we need help …."

Rovers flooded the track with light as they started to surround Cameron and the boys.

"Mate, you'll be fine. We're Rovers and we're here to help. We got Scott's messages and a Blackhawk helicopter is due here any minute now.

"Oh, by the way, I'm Michael Carter from the Blue Mountains Rover Rescue Crew.

"Are any of you hurt? Are all of you, okay?"

Peter took over. "We're absolutely stuffed and need about 20 hours sleep," he said. "We're okay, but our Venturer Leader Mike Hunter and Venturers Scott and Brett need help."

"Who are you?" Michael asked.

"I'm Peter ...'

Michael produced a copy of the Scout Activity Notification form on a clipboard. Another Rover held an umbrella over him as he started checking off names.

"Peter, I have you, what about Mark ..."

"Here."

Michael went through the list of names. He eyed each Venturer as he called their name.

"Are you all okay?"

"Yeah, we're all fine ... thanks," Cameron said.

"Your cooees were terrific and really lifted our spirits. Thank you."

"Mate, you want to believe our collective spirits were raised too when we heard your 'coooees'," Richard, another Rover said.

"Mind you, you need some work on your tune!"

At this a collective laugh rose as the Rovers started taking Cameron's and the boys' packs off them and escorting them up the track to the cars. A makeshift shelter had been erected so the Rovers, Police and Ambulance Paramedics could study maps of the area and communicate by radio back to the School of Arts.

"Cameron, you better come over here first and brief Brett's rescuers before they set off," Michael said.

"We held off sending them out when we heard your 'cooeees'. This way we could find out what specific equipment we would need and find out how Brett is holding up."

Rovers had organised hot chocolate and sandwiches for the

Venturers and Cameron amid sighs of relief and several 'Thank you'. Peter joined Cameron and the pair helped pinpoint exactly where Scott had been keeping Brett tied to the tree. They explained how a pair of peregrine falcons had swooped down to Brett and in a frantic move to protect himself, the boy let go of the abseil rope, pushed away from the cliff and landed back first onto a branch in a tree, thereby impaling himself. The paramedics double checked with Cameron on the condition of Brett; what Scott had done how he was holding up before the group left.

"What's taking the Blackhawk so long to get here?" Mark asked one of the Rovers.

"They were on another task, and it took a while for them to get priority clearance to carry out this job."

"If the chopper is on its way, why do we need the paramedics then? Can't the chopper just lift Brett out and take him to hospital somewhere?"

"No. Winds are still playing havoc with aircraft in the area. No Media choppers have been able to fly because of the winds.

"If the chopper can't get to Scott and Brett, the paramedics must try and get to them by foot to ensure they can stabilise him and ready him for when the helo can lift him out. You must know someone high up in Canberra to have the Prime Minister involved in this...."

"The PM?" Peter chimed in.

"Yeah. Prime Minister Robert Anthony personally authorised the Chief of the Defence Force to use the Blackhawk to help. When we contacted the Commandos, they said they were friends of yours."

The smile on the Venturers almost lit up the briefing area. They never knew Scott's message had got out. They also never knew the PM had become personally involved. Even better, the Commandos they knew were going to be involved.

"We couldn't ask to be in better hands," Ian said.

"I hope not. That's the sort of thing several Media reporters want to hear. They're just down the road a bit and should be here shortly for an update.

"Don't worry. We'll prepare you first."

The boys scoffed down some more hot chocolate and sandwiches. Two Rovers from the Blue Mountains Rover Rescue Crew came and stood with the boys. They said they would help prepare them for any Media interviews.

"Cameron is our spokesman," Ian said.

"He should do the main talking once he's done with the rescue party. We'll just add as required."

Cameron rejoined the Venturers and had a fresh cup of hot chocolate thrust in his hands by a Rover. He was briefed on the Media and said he was ready. Senior Constable Geoff Dobson from the Police Rescue Squad had a few words with Michael Carter. The Police were ready to let the Media down into the area for a news update and for them to interview Cameron and the boys. He also told him the Blackhawk would be landing up the track in 30 minutes in a clearing and he needed help from Rovers with torches. Once the Media found out Cameron and the boys were out of the canyon, they were quick to push the Police and Rovers at the top roadblock for permission to enter the briefing area.

Carter organised for Cameron and the boys to be in front

of several large maps that were placed horizontally on the makeshift briefing area's back wall. The maps had Rover logos on them. A Media conference was called and the various reporters and their camera operators with their cameras, lights, boom extension microphones, tape recorders and notebooks filed in. Michael introduced everyone and gave a brief update of what had happened with Cameron and the boys. He also said the conference could be cut short because of the approaching Blackhawk helicopter and the need to brief the Commandos.

The conference took around 10 minutes with Cameron acting as the Venturer's main spokesman. The boys added what they could and praised Cameron for his cool headedness and getting them out alive. They all praised Scott for his courage in jumping into the tree with Brett and the dangers of trying to keep Brett stable 17 metres from the ground. The Rovers came in for special mention as to their singing, their preparedness, and their ability to pull the rescue attempt together.

Within minutes the sound of the Blackhawk helicopter could be heard. A large group of the Rovers had formed a giant ring around the cleared landing area and shone their torches into the centre. This acted as a fantastic homing beacon for the helicopter crew. The helicopter was buffeted by the high winds and heavy rain and found it hard to land. Initially it was being blown from north to south and then the winds would swirl around to another direction. Finally, the Blackhawk was set down. The Rovers waited until the rotors had stopped swinging before they formed an avenue for the Troopers to walk. Carter was first to meet the two Commandos that alighted from the aircraft.

"G'day, I'm Sergeant Paul Pickering and this is Corporal David Parish," Sergeant Pickering said.

"Which way to the briefing tent?"

Michael introduced himself and the three of them made their way down the track under the camera lights of the Media, towards the briefing area.

"Don't worry Paul. The Media are aware they are not allowed to broadcast your face or details of who you are," Michael said.

"The Police have been briefed and will assist as required."

The throng of Rovers gave way to allow the three men to walk directly to the briefing area. Once inside, it was like old home week.

"G'day Peter. Hi Ian, Mark …." Sergeant Pickering said.

"Long time no see. I notice it wasn't your abseiling that got Brett into trouble …"

"Hi Paul, no it wasn't his abseiling that pinged him. It was a couple of falcons," Peter said.

The Police and Rovers were amazed at the familiarity between the Commandos and the Venturers. Michael and the Police officers walked through what had happened and gave co-ordinates of where Scott, Brett and Mike were located.

"We've sent a ground party ahead to see if they can do anything to help stabilise Brett and ensure the three of them are okay," Michael said. "The party left half an hour ago after Cameron and the boys rocked in. Let me detail their gear and communications."

Michael then set about briefing the two Commandos in more specific terms. A paramedic was assigned to them in case they were able to effect a rescue of Brett so he could start working on the injured teenager instantly he was aboard the helicopter. The Commandos and paramedic made their way back to the aircraft while Rovers again formed a ring of light around the landing area.

Media cameras filmed the aircraft taking off and then beamed the interview with the boys and the Blackhawk to various satellites for instant downloading back in the Sydney newsrooms.

Within 10 minutes the Chief of the Defence Force was on the telephone to the Prime Minister alerting him the news reports were going to air.

Carter tried to get Cameron to take the Venturers home. However, the boys wanted to stay and go home as group when Mike and Scott were out. The boys won and messages were relayed back to their parents.

Helen Robertson was the Group Leader of 1st Hurstville. She had called a meeting of the parents of the missing Venturers and Cameron at the scout hall so they could all watch and listen to the news broadcasts together. This way the group could also be informed simultaneously by the Rovers of what was happening. Helen was relieved and saw the look of worry dissipate when the group watched the news broadcasts of the boys' interviews. The parents were elated when they received calls on their mobile phones from the Rovers the boys would be staying for a few more hours until Mike and Scott walked out.

Allan Morrow had headed off to the Blue Mountains with

his wife Kelly to be near Scott when he was 'retrieved'. The very term 'retrieved' sounded already like something dreadful had happened to Scott. They were keen to link up with Brett's parents. Allan had made a series of calls on his Police radio and mobile phone to Highway Patrol cars along the way to notify them of his movements.

Chapter Eight

Darkness fell silently but surely, and the valley became colder as Scott cuddled Brett closer as the heavy rain and winds kept hitting them. Every so often Brett would let out a murmur and twitch his body. Scott kept talking to him and stroking his mate's face. Mike stood up a couple of times when he heard the various cooees in the valley. He could tell from the sound's weakness the callers were quite some distance away. Scott and Mike had listened hard but could not discern what the noise was as the Rovers broke into song. The winds were too high and carried the singing. They knew it was singing because of the rhythm but couldn't work out from where.

"Mike. Mike. Brett's awake," Scott yelled.

"Ah, great news. Don't let him move too far. Brett, we're with you mate. Hang in there."

Brett had winced, tried to open his eyes and wanted to find out why his back was hurting so much. Scott talked slowly and calmly to his mate and let him know what was happening. Brett started shivering as shock began to set in. The rain had not let up since they entered the canyons. So much for a nice dry day! Scott could only lift one leg at a time to stretch them as he sat straddled on the branch. Brett wanted to stand up but realised he was tied to the tree trunk and going nowhere.

He asked Scott to take the pain away. His whole body was racked with pain as he twisted and tried to get more comfortable. Scott sat Brett more upright. He started to raise Brett's hands slowly from around his neck when his mate cried out loudly in pain and resumed his position of having his hands around Scott and sobbed. The pain was too much and set Brett clutching Scott tighter as his body twitched and writhed. Scott had some hard chocolate in his raincoat pocket he was saving for when Brett was awake. He inched his right hand into the pocket and retrieved the chocolate bar. A few moments later he gave Brett a small square of the sugary substance to suck.

Scott yelled to Mike all that was happening with Brett. It was his way of double checking he was still positioned okay and doing the right thing with Brett. He checked the sling and pad on Brett's back and looked at his hands using his helmet light. They were coloured with blood. He re-tightened the sling amid sobs from Brett. Emotions were running high with Scott as he felt each twitch and movement Brett tried to make. Every move only brought more pain to the boy. Scott was virtually helpless to relieve his mate's pain.

"Try and sleep Brett," Scott said several times to his mate. "Try and think of your own bed, your great mattress and nice pillow. Feel the warmth of your soft blanket and your little dog curled up next to you ..."

It took a little while, but Brett calmed again and drowsed off. Scott was more than ready for sleep too. He feared Brett would wake in fright and have a panic attack, so he didn't dare shut his eyes. Scott gave Mike the thumbs up signal and motioned with his hand under his turned head that Brett was asleep again. Mike replied with his right hand closed and his thumb up. In the distance the growing sound like thunder started to emanate from the southern part of the valley. Mike stood up. He knew this sound.

"Scott. Scott sounds like a military helicopter coming our way," Mike yelled out.

If Scott was dozy before, he was quite awake now.

"Do you think it's a rescue helicopter?"

"The only military ones I'd imagine the Army using in this area are Blackhawks and they're configured for rescues."

"Are they the ones we went through in the simulator at Holsworthy?"

"Yes."

Mike became worried. He looked at Brett and Scott in the tree tied off and wondered how the rescue would be made. The only way would be for a harness to be lowered through the canopy and Brett pulled up. A litter couldn't fit through the tree branches and would be too unwieldy for Scott to manage. The Venturer Leader turned on his helmet light and started waving it slowly in an arc towards where he was hearing the aircraft noise. The rain had eased to the occasional shower, but the winds were still high. The red flashing tail rotor light came into view first as the Blackhawk made its way up the valley.

Mike pointed his helmet light towards the aircraft. He turned it on and off quickly, three times. Then on and off for a longer period before repeating the quick three flashes.

"What are you doing?" Scott asked.

"I'm letting them know via Morse code where we are."

A white light flashed from the side of the aircraft before it changed directions towards Mike and the boys. Both Mike and Scott turned and kept their helmet lights on. The Blackhawk was loud, and the rotor wind shook Scott and Brett. The aircraft turned side on to the cliff and slowly descended. Mike could see the side door open and several people viewing them with night goggles.

Sergeant Pickering and Corporal Parish were assessing whether they could send a line down from a mechanical arm at the outside of the side door or whether a litter would be better. The aircraft was rocking and lifting up and down heavily as the wind gushes and updrafts from the valley played havoc with it. The Blackhawk turned side-on once more, and a large torch shone from inside the cabin at Scott. The torch light slowly followed the path of the main tree trunk up and down and back on Scott and Brett. It then went across to the top of the cliff where Mike was standing and bathed him and the tree he was tied to, in light.

The Blackhawk tried to hover above Scott and Brett's tree but was having too hard a time. It descended opposite Mike and the craft's torch light became focused on a crew member. He pointed to Mike and then closed his right index finger to his thumb in a question of "Are you okay."

Mike replied by pointing to himself and giving the same hand signal. The crew member then pointed to Scott and Brett and did the same. Mike pointed to Brett and then turned around and put a small branch to his back. He then pointed to Scott and gave the okay signal. The Blackhawk crewman acknowledged Mike with a thumbs up sign. He pointed to his watch and then put up two open hands indicating 10 minutes.

Mike showed the okay sign with his open hand and right index finger on top of his thumb … the same as a diver would. The Blackhawk picked up in noise as it ascended from its position and flew back along the valley.

"What the hell was that about?" Scott asked.

"I think he was trying to tell us he couldn't make the lift of Brett without hurting him because of the high winds. Something is going to happen within around 10 minutes. I'm not sure whether he means ground rescue will arrive or he will be back. We'll have to wait and see."

Mike kept looking around to check where the boys had exited the second canyon. He couldn't see any lights, nor could he hear any voices. Scott checked Brett again. His mate was breathing in a shallow fashion, he was pale, and blood still seeped from his wound. Scott was worried for Brett. He had done all he could within his power and yet the light within his best friend was dimming. Brett seemed as if he had started to give up and accept his situation as fate, rather than something that could be fixed, if he was airlifted out. The Blackhawk helicopter was designed to carry four injured passengers on litters hooked to the centre pole in the main cabin, yet it couldn't manoeuvre to pick up Brett. Was it a good choice to send it in as a pseudo-rescue craft?

Scott took solace that at least authorities knew there was a problem at the canyoning site and were trying to fix it. He kept talking to Brett and letting him know what was going on without trying to become emotional. This was not easy. Scott wanted nothing else than for Brett and himself to climb down the tree and for the three of them to walk out and drive home. Something grabbed Scott's attention and he turned to face where he and the other Venturers had exited the second canyon and walked down to the abseil point. Dim light started appearing up the canyon alleyway and dull voices could be heard. Scott looked and thought it was like a scene out of a cartoon about the seven dwarves, with mechanical noises being heard and shadows of people being cast on the opposing rock walls.

Scott told Mike what he saw and heard. Mike looked behind and watched the light display as it kept unfolding, slowly.

"Hey Brett, looks like we have some company," Scott said quietly into Brett's ear.

"It's quite funny what I see. It looks like something out of a major cartoon. If I hear people singing, I'll freak."

Mike now focused on the last canyon exit point. He too could see the dim lights and hear mechanical noises.

"Scott, if this is a ground rescue party then within two hours, we should be having some nice hot coffee with Cameron and the others," Mike said.

"If it's not the ground rescue party, then by God, they soon will be."

Scott smiled as he relayed what Mike had said to Brett. The injured boy grimaced and then said softly: "Thanks, Scott. I won't forget you."

A tear made its way down Scott's cheeks. He was with Brett because there was no one else who could do the job. Also, by choice, Scott had abseiled and climbed into the tree and administered rudimentary first aid to his best friend. Brett would do the same for Scott. They were mates. Lights and voices started making their way down the high walls of the exit point. Both Mike and Scott instinctively turned on their helmet lights.

"At last, we found you!" one of the search party members yelled out.

"It's great to see you," Mike replied.

The party of eight made their way to Mike.

"Hi, you must be Mike Hunter? I'm Bruce Dryden and here we have members of the Blue Mountains Rover Rescue Crew, a paramedic, and an arborist."

"Excellent. We'll need every one of you to help the boys and get Brett to safety."

Mike introduced himself to each of the party members and then they all put their torches onto the tree and the two boys.

"Mike, this is Tim who is a tree climber or arborist by trade," Bruce said.

"I'm pretty sure we can lower Brett down without too much difficulty," Tim said as he surveyed the scene. "I'll have to get a line in the branch above the boys and then climb up and tie off. Once that's done, I can lower myself down to Brett and tie him into my harness.

"The rest is easy as I lower him down to our paramedic who will be at the bottom by then."

"What happened to the Blackhawk?" Mike asked.

"The crew thought it too risky to attempt the rescue for fear of further damaging Brett if he got buffeted by the winds and pushed back and forth into other branches," Bruce said. "That said, they have returned to where your cars are and are waiting for us to signal them to come back and pick up you three."

Tim got to work straight away. He yelled to Scott what he intended to do and for him to shield Brett in case a rope he was throwing missed its mark and hit the boys. While Tim was organising his rope and harness, a female paramedic abseiled down another abseil rope to the bottom. She was followed by two of the Rovers.

Tim had a small ball with a light rope attached which he threw into the tree fork about two metres above the boys. The ball went sailing through the fork and dropped down just above Scott.

"Don't grab for it yet Scott. We don't want you overbalancing and falling out now," Tim said.

"Okay."

Tim jiggled the line and the ball fell within Scott's reach.

"Okay Scott, grab the ball and pull the line through slowly," Tim said.

Scott got the ball and started pulling the line down. It soon joined a thicker rope like the abseil rope. The teenager worked the rope until he had hold of the thick rope.

"Alright Scott, just pull down a bit further. That's it. Hold it there. Now, I want you to pull the line up to yourself until you have the ball."

Scott was starting to wonder where Tim was going to go with the ball and rope.

"Steady yourself in the tree and see if you can throw the ball to me," Tim said.

Tim had replaced Mike at the cliff ledge abseil tie off point and was tied off to the prussick loop.

"Okay mate, let's play catch."

Scott was not a ball thrower. He was not exactly the world's most coordinated teenager either. However, he managed his way through activities and tried his best. The first attempt to throw the ball to Tim failed. Scott pulled down some more rope and shifted his sitting position slightly. The second attempt was right on the money. Tim caught the ball and started to haul the line to himself and then the larger, thicker rope.

Mike, Bruce, and the others stood ready to assist but let Tim do the work. Below, the paramedic and Rovers had built a portable stretcher from materials they had with them. The rescue attempt was working, slowly. The rain started easing and the winds began to abate. Tim kept pulling the line until the larger rope reached him. He undid the smaller line and attached a karabiner to the free end of the rope. Tim then slid the metal device over the main line of rope. Now the two parts of the rope were connected. Tim pulled on the main body of rope and the karabiner slid up the rope until it reached the fork above Scott and Brett.

"Don't worry Scott, that's my line to climb up above you. I'll then re-configure it and come on down to you and Brett. Okay?"

"No probs."

Tim uncoiled the rest of his rope that was attached to Scott's tree. "Below!" he yelled, so he could alert the Rovers and Paramedic what he was doing. Tim then threw the rope down to the base of the tree. He put his rucksack back on and abseiled to the bottom of the cliff.

Scott put his hands under Brett's shirt and felt around the sling and padding. He then looked at his hands in his torchlight.

Some blood was still seeping out. Hopefully, not long from now the paramedic could better stabilise Brett.

Tim pulled out a pair of orange jumars and attached them to the line of rope running up the tree. The jumars were special metal rock climbing devices named after the Swiss factory that made them. They had a series of teeth on them to allow ropes to pass through them one way and grip on the opposite direction. He connected some prussick loops to the jumars and asked one of the Rovers to hold the rope taught for him as he chivvied up the line.

"Horses for courses," Mike said to Bruce.

"He climbs the rope like he was born to it."

"Our Tim runs a tree lopping type business and climbs up and down trees virtually every day. When Canberra got Scott's message about being in a tree, we were notified to try and find a tree lopper. It just so happens Tim is also a member of our Rover Crew, so we didn't have to look too far, and he was keen to help out."

"We're glad to see you. Any word on Cameron and the boys?"

"Yeah, they're well and truly out and being looked after with hot chocolate and sandwiches. They are all fine."

Mike was glad. He hated to lose control of the Venturers he had tried hard to nurture since they came into his care. He looked at Scott and Brett and gave them the okay sign with his right hand. Scott responded the same. Tim chivvied his way up the tree equal to Scott and Brett in a matter of minutes. He sat complacently in his abseil harness tied off to his jumars.

"Howdy lads," Tim said as he manoeuvred into place.

He kept his distance from Brett and Scott, so he didn't bump them. Tim checked the rope work of Scott and said it looked good and tight.

"Alright I've got to go above you and retie the rope so I can get you two out of here. Hang in there Scott, you too Brett."

Tim then continued chivvying up the rope to the fork above the boys. He climbed into the fork and put a prussick loop around the tree and tied it off with a metal shackle. He then did the same again with a second prussick loop and shackle and connected himself to it. Tim undid his jumars and put them in his rucksack. He was then free to haul the rope up and re-feed it through the top prussick loop and drop the ends down to the two Rovers and paramedic below.

Instinctively, Andrew, one of the Rovers at the base of the tree, tied double figure of eight knots into the ends of the rope to save anyone slipping off them. Tim connected himself to the abseil rope and tied off. He then undid himself from his prussic loop and put it away in his rucksack too. Now he was ready for Brett.

"Andrew, Keith, I'm right to go," Tim yelled down.

"Okay, abseil when ready. We're on belay," Keith, the second Rover at the base of the cliff said.

"Scott, I'm coming down now to get Brett."

"Okay," Scott replied.

Scott leant into Brett and told him what was happening. He said his time in the tree was almost over and he'd be on safe ground soon. Tim abseiled and lowered himself down to the two boys. He tied off his abseil gear.

"Okay Brett, I'm going to get you down now. Just do as I say," Tim said.

Brett was semi-conscious and mumbled something to Scott. The second boy looked at Tim and raised his hands in a sign of 'I don't know what he said either.' Tim manoeuvred himself close to Brett. He found the boy's abseil gear and connected a karabiner to it. Next, he and Scott untied the rope holding Brett to Scott and the tree. Slowly, Tim pulled and positioned Brett into position between his legs and then straightened his legs to keep them both away from Scott and the tree. Tim placed his left hand around Brett's head and with his right hand, undid the tie-off knot one turn. This allowed for a slow progress down the rope where Tim could keep maximum control on Brett.

"Scott, stay where you are until I call you. Will you be able to tie yourself back onto this rope and abseil down, or do you want me to come and get you?" Tim asked.

"I'll be fine. Once you give me the okay, I'll start my way down."

Tim smiled and then started descending the tree with Brett. The injured Venturer was not in good shape. Below him the Rovers and the paramedic had prepared a makeshift stretcher with materials they had brought with them. The paramedic stood anxiously to get her hands on her patient. She knew the nation's eyes were on her and she was ready and equal to the task. Brett's feet touched the ground first followed by Tim. The Venturer was placed in a sitting position while the two Rovers undid his abseil gear to free him from Tim and the rope. They then undid his abseil harness and took it off.

"Alright boys, my turn," Nerida said.

"Place him on his stomach on the stretcher and help me lift his clothes up."

While Nerida and the Rovers were starting to work on Brett, Mike and the rest of the party were making their way down the cliff. Scott watched impatiently as he saw Brett being lowered to the valley floor. Finally, Tim looked up and gave him the thumbs up signal to commence his abseil down. Scott pulled Tim's abseil rope towards him and connected to it before tying off. He then undid himself from the tree and the shorter rope Mike used to set up so he could abseil into the tree.

"Below," Scott yelled as he dropped Mike's rope.

With a few deft hand movements Scott untied his holding knot from the abseil rope and started the short descent down. There were lights moving everywhere. The cliff had Rovers looking over the edge and back up from the bottom. Lights shone around Brett as he lay motionless on the stretcher. It was just lucky the rain had stopped, and the wind had abated a while ago.

Clunk, clunk. Scott finally touched down to the valley floor. He didn't last long as his legs were numb from sitting straddled in the tree too long and he fell over. Both Tim and Mike came racing over to him to see if he was okay. They were greeted by a smiling and laughing Scott.

"Are you okay mate?" Mike asked.

Scott started fumbling with his abseil gear to disconnect himself.

"Yeah, I just fell over as my legs were so numb from sitting in the tree."

"You'll be fine Scott. Just get up slowly when you are ready and have a walk around. It happens to me sometimes too," Tim said.

Mike and Tim hovered around Scott and then helped him stand up.

"You made us all pretty proud of you today," Mike said. "There was no way the tree was going to take my weight and Brett's too. The job fell to you, and you came through. Well done, Scott. It was quite heroic what you did today. I'm sure Brett's parents will be very glad too."

Tim put his hand on Scott's shoulder and broke out in a large smile. "You know we were looking for a gig like this to try out our skills … and you and Brett provided it," Tim said.

"Well done, Scott. A great job. You can canyon with me anytime."

Scott never sought accolades. He did what he had to do without too much thinking. Although Mike and Tim's helmet lights were on Scott's face, they couldn't pick up that the teenager was blushing.

"How's Brett?" Scott asked. "Will he be okay?"

Nerida had finished re-bandaging Brett. She had taken off Scott's sling and pad from around Brett, cleaned up the wound and added a new pad and a bandage. She had also set up a plasma drip being held by Keith.

"He'll be fine it we can get him to hospital pretty quickly," Nerida said.

"He's lost a lot of blood and needs to get that branch out and the wound fixed."

In the background Scott heard one of the Rovers on an emergency radio.

"Zero alpha, this is bravo mike romeo, come in."

The Rover tried a few times before a faint crackle was heard.

"Bravo mike romeo, this is zero alpha, over."

The Rover then gave the all-clear sign for the Blackhawk helicopter to return. In the background of the transmission a loud cheer could be heard as the waiting Rovers, Media, other emergency service personnel and Venturers heard the news. Cameron and the Venturers started dancing as the Rovers formed a ring around them and clapped. Excitement erupted throughout the mountain top as word spread Brett was free from the tree.

Now to get him out.

Chapter Nine

The whole of the rescue party now gathered near Brett as the boy lay still on the makeshift stretcher.

"The next part should be easy as the Blackhawk returns and we have the three of you lifted up and out of here," Bruce said.

"I don't think we'll have time for drop-offs," Nerida said.

"Brett is starting to worsen and needs to get to a hospital immediately."

"Done. Phil, radio Sergeant Pickering and tell him the situation. He has two passengers only – Nerida and Brett," Bruce said.

"Roger that."

Phil took out his radio and called the Blackhawk to alert them of the situation. He then called the main command post and told them of what was happening. Michael Carter called Cameron and told him the news. The Venturers went quiet and retreated away from the main throng of Rovers.

"I hope he makes it," Ian said.

"We all do," Peter replied. "At least they can now get him out of here and to proper medical attention."

Carter relayed the message back to Ben Wolfe and Sergeant Wallace at the School of Arts at Mount Elizabeth. A short Media conference was held by Ben and Sergeant Wallace and the Media became busy with their respective phone calls and pieces to camera.

The weather had settled, and the Media helicopters were allowed to fly into the area. They were ordered to keep away from the Blackhawk and to let it do its rescue with good space around it. Allan Morrow arrived at the School of Arts just as the Media conference began and was able to get a good handle of what was going on. He didn't introduce himself to the Media but to Sergeant Wallace and Ben. Brett's parents Rod and Leonie had arrived ten minutes earlier. The Venturer parents introduced themselves and were briefed in private as to what was happening with their sons. They decided to drive to the top of Alexander Plateau and link up with Cameron and the Venturers.

Nerida kept talking with Brett and various Rovers took it in turns to hold the plastic plasma fluid bottle up so it could drain into the stricken Venturer. The various conversations between the Rovers, Mike and Scott stopped suddenly when they heard mechanical rotor noise from the adjoining valley. It wasn't just one helicopter but three, as two Media aircraft shadowed the Blackhawk from a short distance away.

The radio came back into life and searchlights from the front of the Media aircraft switched on and started scanning the valley until the rescue party was in sight. The Rovers stood back and tilted their heads down so their helmet lights were directly on Nerida and Brett. The Blackhawk hovered around 25 metres above the group and a line with a rescue collar on it started to be fed downwards. Brett's stretcher had already been prepared with a sling from each corner joined to a central ring. Once the helicopter's line arrived, the Rovers attached Brett's sling to a large hook and helped Nerida position the rescue collar around herself.

The Rovers gave the thumbs up and the crewman leaning out of the side door of the Blackhawk returned the signal. Brett and Nerida were slowly lifted above the tree and cliff line and up to the aircraft. Sergeant Pickering and Corporal Parish helped pull the two people aboard and then shut the door. The pilot then flew the helicopter forward and into a tight arc back along the valley.

While the rescue lift was taking place cameramen from both Media helicopters were sitting on the floor of their respective aircraft filming. They were outside their side doors with their feet on the helicopter's skids for balance. The Rovers gave a rousing cheer as the Blackhawk took off and then waved to the Media helicopters before setting off. The Media aircraft turned in an arc and flew back out the valley. Bruce stopped the group and told them what they were about to do.

"We can't go out the short way as it is too dangerous at night and too slippery after all this rain," Bruce said. "If we go out around the valley walls along the river we could be swimming out because of the rain. Virtually, our only option is the way we came in except we can get up and around this last abseil and re-enter the canyon from elsewhere. Are you are up to it?"

Mike looked at Scott and grimaced.

"How about it mate, can you do it? One last big push of exercise and we'll be out of here," Mike said.

"I'll be fine. If I need any assistance, I have all these Rovers to help me," Scott replied with a smile.

"Don't worry Scott. We got Brett out and we'll get you and Mike out," Andrew said.

"Okay, it's settled. Phil, radio in what we're doing and then we'll start our climb out," Bruce said.

Phil cranked up the radio and let the Rovers on the plateau know what was happening. He put the radio back into its cradle on his backpack. Keith led the way as the party rambled over a rocky area before a path could be found that wound its way above the cliff ledge everyone had abseiled earlier. Relief of sorts started to flood over Scott as he was about to pass the abseil point that held his attention for so long. He stopped, pulled out his camera and took some photos of Brett's tree.

He then lay down and crawled to the edge of the ledge and took photos of the falcon's nest. The photos would come in handy later to explain to anyone what happened and why. Scott stood up to put his camera in his pocket and the distant cry of 'kee, kee, kee, kee' could be heard.

"What's that?" Keith asked.

"They're the parents of the eggs in the nest," Scott replied. "They're the ones that flew at Brett causing him to jump backwards into the tree."

"Well, they were only protecting their young. Like what we're doing."

"I hadn't thought along those lines. You're right."

Keith and Bruce led the way back along the now swollen creek line towards the first of three canyons the group had to climb out. There was no easy exit. Every abseil through the canyons down was a climb back up the canyon walls. Rain fell intermittently and was more a nuisance than a real problem

– except for the creeks that were rising in large volume by the hour. The small glen that led to the canyon entrance was eerie now. During daylight the giant twisted tree roots were like ships' hauling lines. However, at night, the roots took on a more sinister look as the helmet lights of Scott and the Rovers seemed to make the roots move and writhe in a slow dance as their lights moved around them. The roots almost came to life as the light and shadows of the party passed over them. Scott almost laughed as the only things missing now were some spooky music and people running from ghouls.

"Just ahead we have the easiest of the canyons to enter," Bruce said. "Nice walk out. However, now we must climb up the inside walls we abseiled down. It shouldn't take long."

When Scott, Mike and the Venturers walked out of this canyon the floor was virtually dry. The walls down were dusty and dry. Now there was a moving carpet of water on the canyon floor as the rain had collected in various rock ledge pockets and spilled out onto the rocky floor. The rock walls were stained with water and dripped in parts where water had fallen through the cracks above.

"I'll chimney up first and set a safety line for the rest of you," Keith said.

"Keep out of the water and keep dry. I should be up the walls in around 10 minutes, or so."

Bruce looked at Scott and Mike. "Don't worry. Keith is one of our best rock climbers. He'll work his way up the narrow cracks to the side of where you abseiled in and then climb out through the small triangular hole above."

"This is where we had a sloping rocky face at the bottom

of the rock wall and a tree with a prussick loop attached, if I remember," Scott said.

"Yes. There is a large sloping rock with a triangular hole at its base you had to climb into," Bruce said. "Then you would have abseiled into the chamber and down to where we are now. It looks different at night, doesn't it?"

"Yeah, I haven't been caving yet, but I imagine it to look very much like this at times."

Bruce smiled and pointed to the two walls forming the canyon.

"Caving is very much like this. Sometimes with a lot of space, almost cathedral like. Other times, so small you can only squeeze yourself through.

"The trick is not to get worried about the rock faces closing in on you. Think positive thoughts and it's amazing what you can achieve as you climb through the narrows."

When Bruce and Scott looked up, Keith was more than halfway up the canyon walls. He had bouldered and chimneyed his way up the rocky walls with ease. Scott shook his head as he watched how deftly Keith moved. Mike placed his hand on Scott's shoulder.

"Don't worry Scott. Keith will drop a safety line down which will make it pretty easy for the rest of us to climb the walls," Mike said.

"This is probably the hardest one to climb. The others will be easier and then we have a nice dirt track to take us back to our cars."

"I guess it just seems daunting because of the dark," Scott said.

"You'll be fine. Remember, just take your time as you prussick up the rope and rest when you need to."

Scott nodded his head in agreeance. Brett was the only one who had problems. The other Venturers were out sipping hot chocolate and eating sandwiches. This would be a small time of exercise on the rope as Scott manoeuvred up the rope and rocky walls. Keith signalled he was about to climb out the small hole at the top. Andrew stood next to Bruce and said he would climb out first to give Keith a hand at the top in case anyone needed a bit of a lift. Within a few minutes light was breaking through the hole from above as Keith looked down.

"Below!" Keith yelled as he threw his climbing rope down through the canyon to the Rovers below.

"Got it," Andrew replied.

"I'll come up next to give you a hand."

"Okay mate. The rope is secured. Start your climb."

Andrew tied his prussick loop around the rope. Bruce and Mike held the rope firm as Andrew started to climb up the walls and pull and push his prussick knot with him. He was like a spider with large legs and easily climbed up the various ledges, nooks and crannies. Within a short time, he was starting to disappear through the small entrance at the top.

"Bruce, best you come up next and then we'll get Scott, Mike and the others."

"Okay."

Bruce tied himself on the rope while Scott and Mike held it taught for him. Bruce was strong and had large hands. He was not the world's best rock climber, but he was sure and steady as he slowly climbed the rope and rocky walls. Scott followed him with his helmet torch as the Rover made his way up the rope. At times the lights of the others on Bruce extended his shadow to around twice his body size. Scott thought it was quite amusing as it reminded him of the movies of sword fighting knights in castles with candelabra and open-hearth fires projecting huge silhouettes of the combatants as they weaved and parried in their dangerous duels.

"Okay Scott, you can start getting ready," Bruce said as he neared the triangular exit.

Scott was now impatient. He wanted to end this adventure and find out what happened with Brett and to link up with the other Venturers.

"Climbing," Scott yelled as he moved his prussick knot up the rope and began his climb out.

Mike and a couple of the other Rovers held the rope taught as Scott pushed and pulled his way up the rope and various ledges. A couple of times the teenager stopped to rest his tired body. He always remembered his father telling him of the various fitnesses people acquire.

"A bicycle rider can be fit for riding bikes all day," Scott's father told him. "Put a fit footballer on the same bike and tell him to ride the same distance and he won't be able to do it. The same applies for the bike rider playing the same game of football at the same level as the footballer. You acquire a different fitness level for different sports. Not all of them cross over."

Scott thought of his dad as he pulled and pushed his way up the rope. He was now halfway up and could see lights and shadows emanating from the exit point. A scraping noise echoed through the canyon chamber and the exit hole suddenly blocked. Scott looked up to see someone falling through the hole. Instinctively, Scott arched himself across the rock wall narrows to fill the space, like what Cameron had done for him at the beginning of this saga.

"Aaagh," reverberated through the chamber as Bruce fell towards Scott. The Rover tried to grab rock ledges on his way down, but his momentum made it impossible for him to grab a ledge and hang onto it.

Bruce fell directly onto Scott's right leg and an audible 'snick' could be heard. He then bounced off Scott and forced the Venturer to slide from between the rock walls to a standing position. Instinctively, Scott pushed his legs and arms out against the wall as the Rover began the last part of his fall. It all happened in milliseconds. The exploding pain in Scott's leg was also enormous as he grimaced heavily, and tears started swelling up in in his eyes.

"Gotcha!" Scott yelled as he grabbed Bruce's abseil harness and hung on for all he was worth. The strain on the teenager was enormous as he grappled with Bruce and tried to hold him around his harness while the Rover regained his senses. Scott was tied off on the rope with his prussick knot and wasn't going anywhere. He tried to manoeuvre Bruce to a small ledge. Once Bruce took control of himself and stood on the ledge, Scott reached over to the Rover and clipped a karabiner from his abseil harness to him.

"You're not going anywhere Mister."

Bruce was trembling. His hands were a mangled mess of abraded skin and blood. Scott recognised the symptoms instantly of the first stages of shock.

"Thanks, Scott. You're bloody amazing," Bruce said through gritted teeth.

Scott slowly put his legs around Bruce so he couldn't move anywhere. He ran his light over Bruce and saw the blood streaming from the Rover's hands.

"It was nothing. I was just hanging around," Scott said haltingly with a smile that hid his own pain.

The boy reached into his pocket and pulled out a clean handkerchief, reached over to Bruce and wrapped the Rover's left hand. He then pulled out his own shirt and tore a strip from the bottom.

"I don't think your mum's going to like you for doing that," Bruce said.

"It's okay. It's for a mate of mine," the teenager said as he wrapped the strip around Bruce's right hand.

"What happened up there?"

"I climbed out of the hole and instead of moving directly away from it I started talking with Keith and Andrew," Bruce said.

"I forgot I had unhooked and was about to move away from the edge when I lost my balance and slipped on the rock and down the hole.

"It was like going down the plug hole in a sink. I honestly believed I was going to die as I couldn't grip any rock ledges.

"Then all of a sudden I felt I was bumping into you."

"You certainly bumped into me alright."

"Sorry Scott. If you hadn't chimneyed up that section of wall I would be dead now. How the hell you grabbed my harness after I knocked you from the wall. I'll never know."

Scott was in a lot of pain with his right leg and slowly shifted his body with a grimace. The youth imagined the pain being like acid poured onto his bare skin.

"I saw you falling, and I guess I instinctively put my legs across the gap between the walls to try and stop you. When you pushed me upright, I just kicked out and grabbed for your harness and was lucky enough to find it in the confusion. Are you okay now? How are your hands?"

"I'm fine, Scott. I'll be okay. Thanks for helping me. That's two rescues in one day. No more, okay?"

"No more. I've done enough for a day," Scott said as he gave out a huge cheesy smile.

Scott looked around and saw a ledge behind him.

"Bruce, do you think you can climb on the ledge over there?"

"I can undo my prussick knot once I'm on the ledge and give it to you to climb out. Once you're out you'll have to tie it on the rope and send it down to me."

"I can do it. We'll both have to manoeuvre to get on the ledge. Come on."

Andrew and Mike had both called frantically to Bruce when he fell. They were in a state of awe as they watched Scott stretch out and take Bruce's fall on his legs. Both held their breaths when Bruce continued to fall. Both had screamed out when Scott had stopped Bruce's fall a second time.

"Holy hell! Did you see that?" Mike yelled out.

"Bruce are you okay? Scott, what about you?"

"Mike, we'll be okay. Bruce has some problems with his hands and will need some help to get out," Scott said.

"Scott, can you put him on your prussick knot? If so, we can start hauling him out," Andrew said from the top of the canyon.

"Yes. Once we both get on top of a ledge, I'll unhook myself and put Bruce on. I'll then wait on the ledge until you send the prussick rope down to me."

"Alright Scott. Keep going."

Scott swung himself and Bruce around to face the wall with the ledge. He helped lift and push Bruce up the wall and tried to climb up to the ledge with the Rover. Every time Scott tried to put pressure on his right leg a searing pain shot through his body. He was almost in tears as he managed to get Bruce and himself over the ledge. The two lay there panting for a few moments while they caught their breaths. Scott checked Bruce's hands and noticed blood was still oozing from under his makeshift bandages. He reached over and tied them tighter to stem the blood flow.

After a few minutes, Scott unhooked himself from the climbing rope and tied Bruce on. He signalled to Andrew that Bruce was ready to climb out.

"Okay Andrew, Bruce is on his way out. He can't use his hands much, so you'll have to help him."

"No worries, Scott. Okay Bruce just use your legs to push away from the opposing wall while Keith and I help haul you up."

"Thanks mate."

Scott watched as Bruce fumbled his way over the ledge and positioned himself on the rope. The Rover tried to help pull himself up but had difficulty. Slowly, Keith and Andrew hauled Bruce up. Scott watched the slow ascent from his lying position. He saw the two helmet lights in the hole and a pair of hands reach down to Bruce when he neared the exit. Scott tried to move and found it extremely hard. He ran his right hand down his thigh and felt for any breaks. No punctures. Just an immense area of pain in his thigh. The Rovers pulled the rope up and tied Scott's prussick loop to it before lowering it down to the Venturer.

"Okay, I've got it," Scott said as he retrieved his loop. He then tied it back on the rope and connected himself to it. It took a huge, concerted effort to push himself off the ledge and into an upright position on the rope. The pain in his leg was so intense he started crying, quietly. Mike watched helplessly as Scott inched his way up the canyon walls. He knew his charge was in trouble. Scott was normally one of the most active members of the Unit. Here, he was gingerly working his way up the rock walls.

"Scott, are you okay?" Mike yelled.

"Yeah, I'm fine. I won't be long now," he said haltingly.

Scott had gritted his teeth and kept trying to move and push his body up the rope using anything he could to help. The exit hole loomed larger, and Andrew's voice could be heard more clearly.

"Nearly there mate. Keep pushing," Andrew said.

"I might need some help getting out."

"We're here to help. Don't worry."

Two pairs of hands reached through the exit and grabbed Scott. The Rovers strength was extraordinary. They pulled him gently through the hole and helped him stand on the slippery rock shelf. The youth then fell uncontrollably as his legs gave way. Scott looked around and saw Bruce sitting near the tree used as the tie off point for the rope and the two Rovers. He looked around and saw a large stick and used it to gingerly stand up and hobbled over to Bruce and leant on the tree.

"How are your hands, Bruce?"

"Okay. How are you going mate?"

"I think I've corked my thigh."

"Corked your thigh, huh? Trying to bottle yourself, eh?" Scott laughed.

"No. I think I bruised my muscle when you fell into me. I'll be okay."

The two 'patients' kept talking as Andrew and Keith organised for Mike and the others to make their way up the rock walls and out of the exit point. Mike climbed as quick as he could so he could get out of the canyon and check on Scott. Normally, the boy would be brimming with confidence and speaking at 1000 miles an hour – a sure sign he was excited by some form of adventure. Instead, Mike watched as Scott had slowly climbed out of the canyon in virtual silence. Mike got his head out of the exit hole and scanned the immediate area with his helmet light. He saw Scott leaning on the belay point tree speaking with Bruce. Scott had been crying with pain.

"Hi guys. How's it going up here?" Mike asked.

Andrew nodded in Scott's direction.

"Don't worry Mike. Our double hero is fine. Just shaken but okay."

"Thanks Andrew."

Mike climbed out of the hole and made his way across the

slippery, smooth rock that led to the belay tree. He cleared the rock and undid his prussick knot.

"Are you two okay?"

"Yeah, I have a few problems with my hands where I scraped them on my way down. However, I'll be okay – thanks to Scott," Bruce said.

"I'm okay. I must have corked my thigh when Bruce fell onto me. I'll be fine."

"Bruce, lucky you had our quick-thinking Venturer with you in the canyon. Can you imagine what would have happened if Scott was not there to fall into?"

"Mike, I don't want to think about it. I know this Venturer has proved he really is a hero today – not once, but twice. I'll always be living testament to that!"

"Bruce, I did what I had to do. I saw a problem and tried to fix it instinctively. I'm not a hero. Just someone who tries," Scott said emphatically.

Keith helped the last of the Rovers out of the exit hole and onto the grassy verge near the belay tree. He took Phil aside and asked him to radio through to the Alexander Plateau and advise them what had happened. Phil was to be specific in how Scott had saved the life of Bruce in the canyon. When Phil pulled out his radio and started to send his message the Rovers went quiet. They listened while Rovers on the Plateau relayed what had happened. Phil was instructed to radio back in five minutes.

Scott was uncomfortable with the fuss around him. He was not a hero. They are people who do extraordinary things in extraordinary circumstances. He had just done what came instinctively to him. Phil turned his radio back on and found it hard to discern what the operator was saying on the other end. Rovers and Venturers alike had started singing out in unison when word spread of what Scott had just done. The Rovers and Venturers formed a ring around the radio operator and started singing.

"Well done, Scott. Well done, Scott!" could be heard throughout the plateau and resonated through the airwaves. Scott turned his face away from the group and hobbled away as if he was going to go to the toilet. Instead, he wiped a stream of tears from his face. He felt embarrassed.

"It's okay mate. We're all so proud of you," Mike said as he sidled next to Scott and put his arm on the boy's shoulder.

"This is a special day for Rovers throughout the State as they came to rescue us. You became a draw card and magnet to the Rovers because you inspired the formation of the Rover Rescue Services. I guess they are pretty proud of you and want to thank you that's all."

Scott wiped his face and looked at Mike through moistened eyes. "Mike, I only did what any other Venturer would do. I'm no hero – just someone who did something to help others, like you taught us."

"Yeah, I know. To the rest of the world, you will always be a hero. I know you'll always be someone I look to with respect."

Scott shook his head and wiped his eyes again.

"Coming from you I really appreciate that."

Bruce and the Rovers saw Scott being emotional and Mike comforting him. They gave the two their personal space for a few minutes.

"Okay everyone, it's time to go. We have two more canyons to go and a walk out on the dirt track to our cars," Keith said.

"We need to keep moving. Look for the end of the little valley we're in and the giant tree root we have to climb as it is our way into the next canyon."

The group gathered and started walking along the dirt track which soon gave way to a fast-moving creek that had formed from the afternoon and night's rain. Scott tried to walk and had difficulty. Mike walked next to Scott and got him to hang onto his abseil harness. Scott's pressure on Mike's harness increased as the walk continued with the boy starting to hobble. The valley walls slowly started to come together as the rainforest-like area sprang up around the group. Twice, two of the Rovers nearly fell into the stream because of the slippery conditions.

"There she is," Andrew yelled out.

He pointed to a flat rock wall ahead of them with a giant tree root the group would have to climb to enter the next canyon. Beside the root a steady stream of running water made its way over a rock ledge and down into the valley. One by one the Rovers climbed the root and disappeared into the canyon.

"You might have to give me a hand here," Scott said to Mike as he looked up at the giant root.

He had found it hard enough to climb down but climbing back up with a leg ready to explode with searing pain was another thing. Andrew had gone ahead and set up a belay line further in the canyon and threw it down to Scott.

"Gab this mate, it will make the climb easier," Andrew said.

"Thanks Andrew."

Scott grabbed the rope and slowly but surely made his

way up the root. Mike tried to climb next to him but couldn't fit. Scott was helped over the lip of the canyon entrance by Andrew. The Rover put his arm around Scott's waist to his right hip and lifted him slightly as they walked into the first chamber. Scott whispered quietly to Andrew.

"Thanks. I'm just a bit sore."

"Mate, we're here for you. Don't worry we'll get you out safely and in one piece."

Andrew walked with Scott to the bottom of the next climb and sat him on a rock to the side of the steady stream of water pouring past their feet. Mike joined them and sat next to Scott and studied the boy's face.

"We can rig a boson's chair at the next couple of climbs and help pull you out, if you like?"

Scott pondered what Mike said for a few moments. Now was not the time to try and climb with a leg that felt disconnected and electric shocks being sent down his nerves.

"Let me try it first Mike. If I can't do it then the boson's chair it is."

"Okay."

"This rescue was meant to get Brett out – not both of us."

'Yeah, but fate has a funny way of playing tricks on all of us."

Keith and Andrew scrambled up the mini-abseil point and into the chamber above to set up the belay rope. Canyoners had positioned some strong logs across the opening of the chamber and left prussick loops tied off around them. The two Rovers took a very short time to set up the belay rope and to feed it down the drop to Bruce, Scott, and the others.

"Okay Bruce, you're next," Andrew said.

"Tie the rope to your abseil harness and try and walk up the wall … we'll do the rest."

"Okay. Thanks."

Scott and Mike helped tie the rope to Bruce's harness. Mike then steadied Bruce and helped lift him to the first rock ledge where he could place his toes. Keith and Andrew came into their own and then helped haul Bruce up the small climb. Scott felt good as he knew there was only one more climb to go before the walking track back to the cars.

"Scott, grab the rope and tie on. You're next," Keith said.

"Okay. Thanks."

"Remember mate, take your time, and yell out if you want assistance. We're here for you," Mike said.

"Thanks Mike."

Scott hobbled slowly to the base of the climb and reached up to a hand hold. Mike then helped lift him to a toe hold on a rock ledge. Scott struggled a bit and Keith and Andrew gently and smoothly hauled him up.

"Got you mate. Hang in there!" Andrew said as he helped Scott over the lip of the climb and helped him to a rock to sit on next to Bruce.

"You two make a great pair," Keith said.

"Never mind we have one last climb and then its all walking back to the car."

Scott cringed when Keith told him about the walk. Andrew noticed Scott's facial expression and knew the boy wasn't telling the full truth about his leg. Mike and the others made their way into the chamber. Andrew asked Scott to check on

Bruce's makeshift bandages and to tighten them. While the boy was working on Bruce, Andrew spoke to Mike quietly and said there was no way Scott could chimney out of the last climb. They would have to rig a boson's chair for him and help haul him out.

"Okay. No problems. Once we're out I'll piggyback him up the track," Mike said.

"Alright you take the first part and the remainder of us will take it in turns to do the rest."

Scott rewound the handkerchief and his shirt piece around Bruce's hands. The wounds had stopped bleeding but required stitching. There was no way Bruce could chimney out with his hands so damaged. He would need the boson's chair too. The other Rovers gathered and were ready for the last push out of the canyon. The chamber ahead was the first one Scott had entered on this odyssey. He had clambered down so confidently, well almost, using his back as support against one wall and his feet and hands against the opposing wall to lower himself down. Now the trick was to get up the wall, climb out of the crack between the rock walls. Keith went ahead and made short work of the chimney out. He disappeared through the crack and up to the overhanging tree to tie on the belay line. Andrew was right behind him. Phil and Mike were next. When the four of them were out, Keith made a boson's chair in the rope and sent it down.

"Bruce, we want you up first and then Scott," Keith said.

"Okay."

Scott helped fit the boson's chair around Bruce and then gave the signal to Keith.

"Bruce, just kick out when you need to keep away from the rock wall and let us do the work," Keith said.

"I hope you can take my weight?"

"Mate you're not as fat as Scott! Oh, sorry Scott, I forgot, you're only half Bruce's weight!"

The Rovers laughed as they started to haul Bruce up the tight chimney. The four of them heaved and rhythmically pulled Bruce slowly up between the rock walls. Once he was near the exit crack Keith tied off the rope and the other three gently pulled him to the surface. Mike helped Bruce out of the boson's chair and then started to lower it to Scott.

"Scott, it's your turn now," Mike said. "It won't take long and then you can have a nice piggyback up the track."

"Thanks Mike. A new leg will be fine."

Scott reached out and grabbed the rope. He slowly and quite painfully positioned himself in the boson's chair and gave the signal to haul. The Rovers found the going easier than Bruce as Scott weighed somewhere around 65 kgs while Bruce was 82 kgs. However, anyone looked at it, the weight of Scott or Bruce was a lot to haul up the chamber and everyone was tired. However, there was now a double new imperative to push themselves hard. They had two people to assist out of the remaining part of the canyon safely.

The rope began to lift and take Scott's weight. He felt a rush to his head as the weight was taken off his injured leg. He found it hard to sit in the chair with his weight on his bottom and underside of his thighs. Scott winced and gritted his teeth. It was almost over.

"Can I help in any way?" Bruce asked Keith.

The Rovers and Mike were slowly hauling Scott up the rock wall. "The best way to help him is to encourage him when he clears the crevice. The boy's in a lot of pain and will need help up the track as we walk up the hill ahead of us and then onto the track," said Keith.

"How about I piggyback him?"

"No mate. The first part is reserved for Mike. When he needs a breather the rest of us will take over. For now, your priority is to look after your hands and keep them from being further damaged. We'll have you fixed up shortly too."

"Okay. Just remember. My shoulders and back are okay. I can help take Scott any time any if you can't."

Scott looked up and saw the rock crevice come fully into view. The lights of the Rovers seemed to dance as he was slowly hauled up between the rock walls. Shadows moved up and down in a sort of rhythmic motion as Mike and the Rovers used a hauling method like sailors from a bygone era to lift their only Venturer with them out of the last canyon. Keith tied off the rope as he saw Scott's helmet light start to exit the crevice. Three pairs of hands then gently pulled Scott up the last bit of wall, over the lip entrance and onto firm ground.

"Welcome back," Andrew said to Scott.

"Thanks. It feels like I've been away for ages."

"When we get you fully out of here you can take off your abseil harness as it is the last you'll need it this trip."

"I'm so looking forward to getting out of it and putting it away."

Mike moved in closer and helped lift Scott to his feet.

"Careful here as we straddle this crack," Mike said. A few

more metres and this part of the trip will be over – now for the walk out."

"Mike I should be fine from here."

"We'll see."

Keith re-coiled the rope and stuffed it back in his rucksack. The others all took off their harnesses and put them away too. Phil pulled out his radio and called in to the Alexander Plateau to let them know they were out. Word spread very quickly around the Rovers and Venturers and several cheers rang out. News Media were quick to update their newsrooms the party would soon be back at their cars for the journey home.

"I'm glad they made it," Ian said.

"Yeah, this will be a tale to tell our kids when we're older," Peter replied.

"Hang on. I'm too young for kids yet. I just want the fun."

"Don't we all. Scott's in for a hard time again when he gets here and the Media see him."

"Yeah but at least, we'll be around to help him out."

"Best we talk to Cameron and see what he wants to do."

"Okay."

Scott tried standing and found it nigh impossible and started to collapse. Mike stood next to him and grabbed him before he went too far.

"Now's the time to take a little ride on my back young man."

"Mike, I'm sorry," Scott sobbed. "I just can't take the weight on my leg anymore."

"That's fine mate. We'll get you through this. I promised you that."

Phil, Keith, and Andrew reached down to Scott and picked him up. They placed him on Mike's back. Scott grimaced as his left leg moved awkwardly and then smiled as he put his arms around Mike's neck for support.

"Thanks guys."

"Mate, it's a pleasure," Keith said. "We only have the hill ahead of us and then the dirt track back to the car. It's almost plain sailing from here."

The Rovers took Mike and Scott's rucksacks before heading out of the small glen and up the hill. The walk was slow as Mike found it challenging to carry Scott. It wasn't that Scott was heavy, but the gradient made the walk slow. Within 20 minutes the group had reached the end of the hill track and stood on a large flat rock overlooking the surrounding valleys. Scott was awestruck as he saw the huge number of lights on the far horizon. The lights looked like an extended football ground at night. The Rovers stood in silence as they took in the view. He leant closer to Mike.

"Do you mind if I let people know we're here?"

"Scott, go for it."

Scott put his hands in front of his mouth and shouted at the top of his voice.

"Cooeeee. Cooeeee."

Scott's voice reverberated around the surrounding valleys. Unexpectedly, the same noise, only fainter, seemed to emanate from the far horizon where the ribbon of lights lit the skyline.

"Did you hear that?" Scott asked.

"Yeah, I think we have some company up near our cars," Mike replied.

"That's not company. It's a jamboree!"

Phil took out his radio and called in.

"We're now out of the canyon and in sight of the far horizon leading to the cars."

"Take your time Phil. We'll have hot coffee, chocolate and sandwiches waiting for you," Ben Wolfe said.

"Oh, tell Mike the Media are very keen for interviews and will be in your face the moment you hit our location."

"Roger. Out"

Scott had heard the exchange and gripped Mike tightly with his legs.

"Mike, not now. Please, not now. I don't want to do any interviews now," Scott said as his voice trembled.

"Don't worry sunshine. You'll be fine. Leave it to me."

Mike swapped with Andrew to take Scott while he carried the Rover's rucksack. The move allowed Mike to fall back a bit and ask Phil to send a message to the plateau control area. The reply came back swiftly.

"Brett has been taken to the Westmead Children's Hospital and is being operated on now," Ben said.

"Scott's parents are up here. Brett's parents were here too but have been taken by Police to the hospital to be with Brett.

"Tell Mike we'll set things in motion for him and to look for Tiny Tom. He won't miss him."

Phil burst out laughing when he heard Ben's message. Tiny Tom was probably the tallest Rover the State had. If the little Rover was around then Mike and Scott had no problems. Mike updated Scott to Brett's condition.

News flashes were being sent on all radio and TV stations

as news filtered out the Rover rescue party was clear of the last canyon and would soon be back at their cars. Prime Minister Anthony had kept on eye on the situation as an aide updated him continuously when further news of Scott came to hand.

Chapter Ten

It had started as a low rumbling noise and then intensified as more voices joined in. Once word the Rover rescue party had cleared the last canyon with Scott and Mike, the car park on the Alexander Plateau erupted into cheers and then song.

Rovers, Venturers, and even some of the Police Officers who were former Rovers joined in a euphoric rendition of the scout campfire song:

'I've got that B.P. feeling ... deep in my heart, deep in my heart ... I've got that B.P. feeling ...'

At first the words were indiscernible. The more the Rovers sang, the more the song's cadence could be picked up. The gait of the Rover rescue party picked up when they heard the singing of their confreres. Smiles were beamed from Rover to Rover. Scott on the other hand had gone quiet. He had started to get cold and clammy and hardly moved as Andrew piggy backed him up the final part of the first hill.

'Cooeeee. Cooeeee.' Could be heard coming from the far horizon where the car park was situated.

"Come on Scott. It's your turn to answer them," Andrew said.

Mike sidled up to Andrew and looked at Scott. The boy was

in a lot of pain and wasn't going to be calling out to anyone. He was as pale as a ghost and had tears trickling down his face.

"I'll do it for him," Mike said.

Mike cupped his hands to his mouth and yelled out at the top of his voice.

"Cooeeee. Cooeeee."

The sound had only started echoing around the valley when a series of replies were yelled from the direction of the car park. Rovers started breaking ranks and heading off down the dirt road from the car park towards the rescue party. The Venturers wanted to join in too but were ordered to stay put. The boys started arguing with the Rovers until Cameron calmed them down. He told them of Mike's message and plea. The Venturers acquiesced.

A steady stream of lights started to break away from the ribbon of light on the horizon and head towards the rescue party. Initially, it looked like a large collection of fairy lights snaking its way down from the car park. The lights grew and took on the appearance of a freight train that stretched all the way back to the horizon. A series of twinkling rescue lights could be plainly seen in the bush hundreds of metres away. A giant cheer erupted from the freight train ahead and kept working its way back to the top of the horizon like a Mexican wave.

The Rovers erupted into cheers when the silhouette shapes of the rescue party came into view. Whistles and clapping erupted everywhere as the two parties met and shook hands. Rovers surrounded the rescue party and took their packs and gave them fresh drinks and snacks. A huge shape of a man made his way through the rescue party to Andrew and Scott. He picked up Scott like he was a rag doll and gently placed him on his own back.

"Come on little fellow. We've got you now," Tom said.

Scott whispered his thanks and buried his head into the shoulders of this bear of a man. Tiny Tom strode forward, and the human freight train parted to let him walk through. Hand after hand patted Scott as he and Tom made their way through the crowd. A continuous clapping of hands echoed along the path as Tom and Scott made their way forward. Phil walked up to Mike and said the ploy was ready to be enacted. A surge of Rovers from the control point snaked its way to the rescue party. Tom gently put Scott on Mike's back and had a young Rover sit on his shoulders. While Tom and the others walked to a small clearing before the car park, Mike and Scott made a beeline to the parked cars. Rovers started shouting their tribute to Scott and the other rescuers. In rousing choruses, they shouted B-R-A-V-O-O-O. The young Rover and Venturers all responded in the traditional manner. They hit their closed fists against their opposing hands and stamped their feet yelling T-A-R. Ta.

Reporters and their camera operators made their way to where the Rovers began tossing the young Rover in the air and then catching him. A series of cheers rang out as the play act continued.

Mike saw Allan and Kelly and went straight to them. They quietly nodded to each other and walked down the line of cars to the Morrows'. Mike gingerly put Scott on the rear seat and the boy's mother sat on the other side. Allan got behind the wheel. Mike got into the front passenger seat. Phil watched as the Morrows and Mike headed to their car and then radioed into Ben. Several Rovers started their cars and formed up behind the Morrows in a convoy. The ruse didn't work long but caught the Media by surprise. They were very keen to interview Scott, the hero of the day and find out his story of bravery. They were left with interviewing Andrew, Keith, and the Venturers. Cameron and Peter had been told of the ruse by Phil. They watched the events with interest and laughed when they saw it play out.

"I guess I get to drive Mike's car home," Peter said.

"Yeah, once we can clear ourselves from this overcrowded car park and escape," Cameron replied.

The Media had followed the Rover surge and tried to get into a circle where Tom and some others were throwing around a young Rover. When it was discovered, the Morrows had left the Media made a scramble of their own but got caught up in a continuous line of cars driven by Rovers along the one way track off the Alexander Plateau. Allan Morrow used his mobile phone to call a couple of his Highway Patrol friends and a car was waiting to escort them at the bottom of the Zig Zag railway. Kelly had felt Scott's thigh and reeled when the boy yelped in pain. Scott then lost consciousness. He knew he was safe; his job was done and he was with his family.

Even with a police escort, the Morrow's trip to the Children's Hospital took around an hour. Police had radioed ahead to alert staff Scott was on his way and needed triage assessment quickly. They also wanted a private room to be set aside for the Morrows and Mike. Once the Media became mobile, they rang and radioed their respective newsrooms. A few fresh crews were sent to wait outside the hospital in case they caught a glimpse of the Morrows and Scott.

Allan drove into the emergency area and several film crews were filming his arrival. A Highway Patrol Officer kept the Media back as Allan got out of the car and walked to the other side where Scott was situated. Mike had opened Scott's door and was about to reach in and lift him out.

"Mike, it's my turn now," Allan said. "You've carried him enough tonight and his mother and I will be eternally grateful. I will, however, need a hand with the car."

"No probs."

Mike got into the drivers' seat and drove off to park the car, leaving the Morrows to carry Scott into the triage area. Prime Minister Anthony had been informed of Scott's arrival at hospital and ordered an aide to keep a check on Brett and Scott's conditions. He wanted to see the boys the first chance available. Mike joined the Morrows in a private room and waited for news. It didn't take long. A nursing sister with a clipboard entered the room.

"Mr and Mrs Morrow, I'm Sister Shirley. Scott has been to X-rays and they show he has a fracture to his right femur and will need an operation to set his leg.

"How he walked, crawled and climbed out of your canyon is beyond me as he would have been in immense pain."

Sister Shirley and the Morrows looked directly at Mike.

"What can I say? His heart is bigger than the legendary Phar Lap – our country's best ever racehorse. He did what he felt he had to do for as long as he could. I guess the moment he felt safe in your arms was the trigger for him to switch off and shut down."

Sister Shirley continued. "Anyway, he's in being prepared now for theatre and will be operated on shortly to fix his fracture."

Mike stood aghast when he heard the news. He then realised what Scott had tried to do. The boy did not want any focus on him and walked in extreme pain rather than be carried and had a fuss made over him. Mike knew the boy had problems when Bruce landed directly on him. He knew from the way Scott had hung on to his harness to walk that all was not well with him. However, Scott kept saying he was fine. Mike now knew this was a vain attempt to swing attention from him. Mike asked about Brett and what had happened.

"Brett should make a full recovery too," Sister Shirley said. "He's upstairs in another department but I understand he was operated on within a short time of arriving by helicopter. Surgeons removed the remaining part of the branch and have operated to repair his surrounding organs."

Mike was relieved. He left the Morrows and made his way upstairs and found Brett's parents. They were very glad to see him and wanted to know all the news on Scott.

"Mike, ever since we got here the ward TVs have been running news items of the dramatic mountain rescue of Brett," Rod said.

"While Brett was being operated on, we started hearing news Scott had been involved in a second rescue and may have been injured too. What happened?"

Mike saw the anguish on both parents faces. He sat down

and told them the story of what happened with Brett and the bird strike; Scott's heroic attempt to save their son and the arrival and help of the Rover rescue team. He went into detail of the Commandos in the Blackhawk and how they lifted Brett up from the valley floor and took him to hospital. Mike then swallowed hard and told what happened to Scott when Bruce fell and how the boy had effected a second rescue and was now paying the price.

"Brett was operated on some time ago and is in the recovery ward," Leonie said.

"We expect him here pretty soon."

Both Rod and Leonie put their arms around Mike and hugged him.

"Thank you for helping our son," Rod said.

"Thank you for giving him and the rest of the Unit the training they needed to help each other. Without it, Brett could well have died a horrible death tonight."

"Brett, Scott and the other boys love adventure as you two well know," Mike said.

"My idea has always been to temper the enthusiasm and adventure with the knowledge and training for emergencies we never want to happen.

"We were lucky tonight. Our training paid off."

"Yes. Also, if it wasn't for you and Scott running that campaign about the Rover Rescue Service, things may have been different," Rod said.

"Scott hit on a good story and concept. He had heard the Rovers arguing about it and wanted to do something to help others. If he hadn't come up with the concept and done his research, my paper would never have been involved. Again, we were lucky."

"Mike, maybe it was pre-ordained," Leonie said.

"Maybe Scott knew something was going to happen and took the steps beforehand to ensure when that something took place, he was covered and those around him."

"I know Scott is perceptive about a lot of things, but probably not that *au fait* with all things future."

"Don't know Mike. It's just a woman's intuition about the boy. Anyway, I'm glad all the building blocks were in place, otherwise, as Rod says, we could have been in a different place viewing Brett."

Mike looked at both parents. They had tears of gratitude in their eyes. They gave him another communal hug and sat in silence for a few moments to let the emotional experience linger longer. A nurse entered the room and gave the trio the good news.

"Brett's doing fine. He's just warming up after the operation and once his temperature is within normal bounds we'll move him up here," she said.

Mike and Brett's parents grabbed each other again.

"I better let the Morrows know the good news about Brett," Mike said.

"Give them our love," Leonie said.

"Once Brett is here and all is well, we'll try and link up," Rod said.

"Okay folks. See you soon."

Mike walked over to the lift and pushed the button. The lift was five floors up and would take a few moments to arrive.

He looked out the windows and saw several TV outside broadcasting vans parked outside. He also saw some small cars with radio station markers on them. The lift doors opened, and Mike went down to where the Morrows were waiting for Scott.

"Any news on Scott?"

"No. Not yet," Allan said.

"The hospital had a problem finding a bone specialist that was free to operate. All we know is he is in theatre."

"Allan, we have another problem brewing outside which we will have to address shortly."

"If it's the Media, I know. The hospital staff has been keeping me informed."

"We should hold a Media conference and that way they'll leave."

"Alright, but I want to speak too."

Mike nodded. He understood the Police Inspector father may have some words he would want to say on behalf of his son Scott. When Scott helped rescue his Venturers from the Russian Mafia drug thugs the preceding Christmas, Allan left all Media interviews to Mike. Now he wanted to step up to the plate.

"I'll go down and suss out what's happening. It would be good if you requested a Police Media Supervisor to assist you. This way, there is better control, and we could have the conference on the footpath opposite the hospital and away from the emergency staff."

"Consider it done. I'll make the call. First, tell us about Brett."

Mike told the Morrows what was happening to Brett and then went to a nurse's station in the ward. He placed a call to the hospital's administrator and told him what he proposed.

The Chief Medical Officer was glad to hear from Mike and said his staff would co-operate fully with him. He then explained Prime Minister Anthony's office had been in touch several times to enquire about both boys. He said the PM was anxious to meet with them the following day when they had settled from their surgery. Mike smiled. This night was larger than a Cecil B. de Mille movie extravaganza.

Mike went to the front of the hospital and was met by a barrage of reporters, some who knew and worked with him. He explained a Media conference would soon be held on the footpath opposite the hospital and that Scott's parents would be present. An update to the boys' conditions would be given and some breaking political news. He refused interviews until the Media conference and headed back inside the hospital. It didn't take long before Sergeant David Gallant from Police Media arrived at the hospital and linked up with the Morrows. He was impressed with Mike's handling of the Media so far and was keen to assist both families.

"A small Media conference was held at the Mt Elizabeth School of Arts after you had left the Alexander Plateau," Sergeant Gallant said.

"Who ran it, the Police?" Mike asked.

"No. Ben Wolfe from the Rover Rescue Service was the spokesman I believe. He did pretty well. Ben gave a small breakdown of what happened and how you had to take Scott to hospital.

"Ben also detailed what the Rovers involvement was in the rescue operation and praised the other emergency services for their help and co-operation. You would have been proud of him."

"What about Police? Did they do any interviews on the rescue?"

"No. We have been told to keep in the background on this one and let the Rovers take the running. Sort of make it their own baptism of fire."

"I am impressed. Please pass my thanks to the Commissioner for allowing the Rovers to work their way through this. It is important they take the running and receive the necessary kudos."

"No probs Mike. Now about this Media conference."

Mike and Allan said they were prepared to hold the conference once doctors had confirmed all was well with Scott and Brett had been taken to a normal ward.

They didn't have to wait long. A groggy Brett was wheeled into the empty bed space where his parents had been waiting. He had a few tubes coming out of his nose and back, looked pale but was otherwise in reasonable shape, considering what he had been through.

News of Scott filtered back to the Morrows shortly afterwards. The boy's leg had been operated on and he was in a full leg cast to help prevent movement. Scott would be in a normal ward within the hour. Mike made one more phone call.

Chapter Eleven

Mike's Media conference took place as most people were sitting down for their breakfasts. It had been a long night and an even longer day the day before. Sergeant Gallant called the Media together. He was joined by Brett and Scott's parents, Mike, and Bruce. The Rover rescuer had been to the local Katoomba Base Hospital in the Blue Mountains and had both his hands stitched. Several other Rovers involved in the rescue joined in.

"Ladies and gentlemen, before we start any interviews, Inspector Morrow would like to make an opening statement on behalf of the parents of the two injured boys," Sergeant Gallant said.

Allan stepped up to a mark on the ground the Media had placed so he was in focus with their various cameras. A few radio reporters stayed out of camera shot but extended their hands holding microphones towards him. A couple of newspaper reporters did the same.

"My name is Inspector Allan Morrow from the Sydney Highway Patrol," Allan said. "My son Scott and his best friend Brett were among a group of Venturers led by Mike Hunter and Cameron Wagstaff yesterday when they went to Thompsons Canyon in the Alexander Plateau.

"The group suffered some unexpected circumstances that saw Brett impaled in a tree and Scott trekking through a canyon with a broken leg with his rescuers.

"I'll leave the details to Mike Hunter to tell you. However, on behalf of Brett's parents, Rod and Leonie and my wife Kelly and I, let me tell you we fully believe our boys' rescues were really carried out professionally. Mostly when we hear of mountain rescues, the Police and other emergency services are involved as they were with this one.

"However, the Rover Emergency Rescue Service swung into action within a short time of being called and performed a virtually faultless rescue of our sons. Yes, the Police and emergency services were on hand and assisted but played a secondary role to the Rovers.

"These fine young men and women have trained hard over the last few months in rescues and underwent their baptism of fire yesterday. Their training paid off when they flawlessly retrieved Brett from being impaled in a tree and had him lifted into an Army Blackhawk helicopter.

"Our heartfelt thanks go to Prime Minister Robert Anthony for his personal intervention and authorising the Chief of the Defence Force to give the all-clear for Commandos and their Blackhawk to fly in the valley and pick Brett up.

"It was a dangerous flight in most trying weather conditions and really tested the Army pilots' skills. The Venturers had trained with the same Commandos earlier in abseiling techniques thanks to Mike Hunter. Circumstance brought them together again yesterday with a good outcome and I thank them for their own bravery.

"Both Brett and Scott are now on the mend thanks to the wonderful doctors and nursing staff here. Brett and Scott are expected to make full recoveries."

When Allan Morrow finished speaking there was a moment's silence. Someone at the rear of the conference started clapping and it spread throughout the whole group as they were all moved emotionally by what Allan had to say.

Mike stepped up next and introduced Bruce with his two bandaged hands. He detailed the training the boys undertook before they went canyoning. Then he detailed what happened. He heaped high praise on the Rovers for their fantastic efforts.

Mike then paused. He looked down at the ground while he gathered his emotions.

"I now want to tell you a story about a boy who doesn't want to be called a hero but is everyone's hero today.

"Let me tell you about a Venturer who underwent the hard rigours of training before the canyoning trip and then without hesitation not once, but twice, saved people in life threatening situations.

"I'm referring to Scott Morrow. The same Venturer who last year saved me and the rest of the Venturer Unit from a group of highly dangerous and armed Russian Mafia drug smugglers."

Mike detailed how Scott had volunteered to abseil into the tree to save Brett; how he had found the inner strength to break the thick branch that impaled his mate and then nursed and looked after him until help arrived.

The sound of Mike speaking and the occasional vehicle passing by were all that could be heard. The Media were in rapt attention at what the Venturer Leader was saying about his charge. Mike went on to detail how Scott had saved Bruce and then walked and climbed through the canyons with a fractured femur because he didn't want any fuss from his rescuers. A series of questions and answers followed from reporters keen to get specific angles on what had happened, and the role Scott played.

Bruce weighed in with his praise of the boy he had come to save but instead, had saved him from certain death. He was also thankful on behalf of all Rovers across Australia for the national emergency rescue scheme Scott was instrumental in setting up. At the end of the Media conference, Mike told the news Prime Minister Robert Anthony would be visiting the two boys the following day if they were up to it.

The Media had been ingratiated with details of one of the country's most intriguing rescues. They ran stories of the unsung hero called Scott Morrow who would hold an audience with his country's Prime Minister the next day. Scott was being earmarked for all sorts of awards. The story was beamed around the globe as news houses devoured the feel-good story. Canadian TV stations were keen to link with their Australian affiliate stations and get as much as they could from the Rovers and emergency services personnel.

Prime Minister Anthony's aide confirmed details of his visit with the hospital for the next day. Selected Media only were allowed in to cover the visit and interview the two boys. Mike was busy. He had waited until both Scott and Brett were awake and stayed a short time with each boy and his parents. He then went home and met up with Cameron and his Venturers after some well-earned sleep. They had a few things to plan.

Bruce was in touch with Ben and several Rover Crews around Sydney. There was an opportunity not to be missed.

Scott and Brett had spent a semi-comfortable night in hospital after their respective operations. Nursing staff organised for the two boys to be reunited in a spare ward for the PM's visit. Outside the hospital a group of around 50 Rovers including Bruce and Ben, were in their dress uniforms waiting for the PM to arrive. Mike joined them in his Venturer uniform, wearing his trademark lemon squeezer hat.

"I rang the PM's office and told them what we planned to do so there were no surprises," Bruce said.

"I'm glad mate. You don't need the PM's security staff getting skittish if you jump out and want to shake the PM's hands. Not that you could."

The Rovers then raised a large banner a group of them had made overnight. Mike's eyes watered. 'Well Done, Scott' was emblazoned in giant letters across the banner.

"I thought you'd like it," Bruce said. "We noticed what your Venturers did at Scott's Queens Scout and bravery award presentation last year.

"We figured it was time to revisit the sentiments."

"Mate, you have hit the nail on the head. He'll be thrilled. That is, after he gets over being embarrassed."

"I also have three special presentations to make. The first of course to the PM and the same to Scott with a special one for Brett."

"Well done, Bruce. You're getting good at this."

Several Media crews had turned up and filmed the Rovers waiting for the PM. Mike got a mobile phone call.

"Okay, Bruce, he's two blocks away," Mike said.

"What the ... Who is ...?"

"The PM is on his way. The escort is just up the road."

No sooner had Mike spoken when his Venturers were seen marching up the road from the opposite direction. Peter proudly carried the Unit's maroon flag with its green lettering and Venturer symbol. The boys were all turned out immaculately in their blue and white Venturer uniform and marched into position in front of the Rovers. The Media were actively filming. When the Unit halted Ian shouted out the next command.

"1st Hurstville Venturer Unit what do we give Scott Morrow?"

As one, the Unit struck their fists into their opposing open hands and stamped their feet while shouting out B-R-A-V-O-O-O. The Rovers clapped and cheered and joined in.

"Rovers. What do we give Scott Morrow?"

The voices were stronger and deeper but said the same as the Venturers with gusto. B-R-A-V-O-O-O. Scott and Brett had watched the proceedings from a TV set above their beds. Sky TV was broadcasting the event live. Both boys reached out to each other and held hands for a few moments in a gesture of moral support to each other. Their parents stood beside their beds.

The PM's police escort came into view and worked its way down the street to the hospital. Ian, Ben, and Bruce made their way onto the opposing footpath and waited. The PM's car drew to a stop and Ian opened the front passenger seat door and saluted. Ben and Bruce stepped forward and saluted the

PM who returned the salute as a scout with his right hand at half salute and his thumb holding his little finger. Before the two Rovers could speak, Mike got the Rovers and Venturers into action.

"Rovers and Venturers, what do we give the Prime Minister?"

This time both groups joined as one and shouted out their scouting salutation B-R-A-V-O-O-O. Prime Minister Robert Anthony was emotionally moved. He raised his hand and faced the uniformed group and loudly said T-A-R, ta. He smiled and was about to enter the hospital when Bruce approached him closer.

"Sir, on behalf of the Australian Rover Emergency Rescue Service we would like to make you an honorary Rover in recognition of how you helped Scott Morrow and our Rovers recently," Bruce said.

He then presented the Prime Minister with a special Rover scarf and woggle, stood back, and saluted.

The PM felt the scarf and then saluted Bruce. He was chuffed and broke out in a huge smile. News crews pushed even closer to film.

"Thanks Bruce. I have never met such a dedicated group of young men and women who have trained so hard and then placed the training at the disposal of the community," the PM said. "I will treasure the scarf always and thank you for your sentiments."

Mike hadn't finished yet. He started the next move by clapping and cheering. The Rovers and Venturers followed suit and then gave the PM three loud cheers. The PM acknowledged the sentiments and made his way into the hospital. He was met by the Chief Medical Officer and State Minister for Health who accompanied him to Scott and Brett.

The boys were half-sitting up in bed and noticed a flurry of people coming up the ward passageway. Aides held the door open as the PM and his entourage entered the ward. He shook the left hand of each boy and showed them the special scarf and woggle the Rovers had presented him. Both boys smiled broadly. The PM spent around 30 minutes talking with the boys and their parents. He then told Scott the Governor-General would be in touch with him shortly.

"You are a special youth who I know doesn't want to be called a hero," The PM said to Scott while the Media filmed. "All Australians salute your courage and tenacity and thank you for your bold efforts in saving young Brett here and Bruce from Rovers.

"Your efforts in saving your fellow Venturers and leader from a group of highly armed and dangerous drug criminals last Christmas earned you your State's highest civilian bravery award.

"In recognition of your spectacular efforts in saving Brett and Bruce, you have been chosen by Federal Cabinet to be Australia's first Young Citizen of the Year.

"This will be marked at a special ceremony at Government House in Canberra once you are back on your feet."

Kelly almost choked Scott as she squeezed him hard around the neck when the PM made his speech. Scott was in awe as the Prime Minister spoke. He choked back tears and clenched his fist under the bed clothes. There was nowhere to run.

The State Minister for Health, the hospital's Chief Medical Officer congratulated Scott and shook his hand. The PM turned to go and took a few steps to the door. He turned to ensure the cameras were off and then walked back to Scott. He reached into his suit coat pocket and pulled out a letter.

"This is off the record Scott," the PM said quietly and winked at the boy. "Some friends of yours wanted me to give you this."

The PM gave Scott the letter and left. Only the two boys and their parents remained in the room. Scott looked at the yellow buff envelope. On the top left corner were the words 'Department of Defence. 6th Commando Regiment.' Scott carefully opened the letter. It bore the symbol of a boomerang with a sword facing downwards through it. Under the logo were the words *'Strike Swiftly.'*

Scott read the letter aloud.

'Dear Scott,
BZ.
P.J. Pickering CSC
Sergeant
Bravo Coy
6th Commando Regiment'

Scott couldn't work it out. He passed the letter to his parents and then Brett and his parents. All were in the dark. While everyone talked about the letter and the visit a lemon squeezer hat appeared in the ward window as Mike made his way into the room. Scott and Brett broke out in huge grins when they saw their Venturer Leader. Scott showed him the letter and asked him what it meant. Mike scanned the page and then laughed out loud.

"Our Commando friends have paid you a very high compliment indeed," Mike said.

"In the armed services, especially the Navy, BZ or Bravo Zulu, means job well done. It is also a salute to courage. This is a very special letter that few would ever receive from the Commandos."

Scott was ready to lose it emotionally. Mike walked closer and told him he had brought some people to see him and Brett. A few moments later Venturers from the boys Unit entered the ward. The boys laughed and joked their way through the re-telling of the canyon trip from all perspectives. It was the nursing staff who broke up the party after 15 minutes saying both boys needed to have their rest and quiet time. Mike led the Venturers away and left the boys to their families.

Ward orderlies returned the boys to their wards. Brett was in a lot of pain from sitting up so long and needed to rest and sleep. Scott too was in pain as nerves told him his leg had been interfered with and needed rest. Allan and Kelly left Scott to sleep.

The boy closed his eyes and in his own privacy cried an emotional release he had needed for some time.

Chapter Twelve

Over the next month, Scott and Brett had gone leaps and bounds with their fitness and recovery. Brett was walking around, attending school and Venturers as a passive member. Scott was full of energy but walking with the aid of crutches as the plaster was not due to come off for some time.

Once he left hospital Scott had conducted a series of Media interviews, all the time praising the professionalism of the Rover Emergency Rescue Service. He was also thankful for the great support from his parents, fellow Venturers and Mike. He was a good Media subject. Scott was good looking, a good conversationalist, dressed well and was not only polite but also humble. Mike had prepared him well with Media training and it showed.

All was quiet in the Morrow household until a letter arrived for Scott. It was in a white envelope with the colour logo of a sprig of wattle and a crown on top. It had the words 'Office of the Governor General of Australia' in the top left-hand corner and was addressed to Scott. Inside, Scott read the invitation asking him to go to Government House for a special awards ceremony. He was to be made Australian Young Citizen of the Year. The PM had kept his word.

Scott was quick to show his mum and then telephoned his father at work and to let him know. After all, it's not every day the Australian Head of State invites you to Yarralumla, the official Canberra residence of the Governor General.

Once Mike was told of the invitation date he spoke with his Chief of Staff at his newspaper and arranged to cover the awards ceremony. This was to be a follow-up to the Rover Emergency Rescue Centre story he first covered all those eons ago with Scott before the canyon rescue drama. He didn't tell Scott he'd be there, after all some things had to be a surprise. The Morrows drove to Canberra, the nation's capital, the day before the ceremony and stayed in a motel for the night. This way, they would be fresh for the ceremony and not have to worry about traffic. Mike had done the same but stayed in a different motel. Scott was freshening up his Venturer shirt with an iron when his mother stopped to look at him.

"I remember this scene when we went to Government House in Sydney for your Queens Scout and Bravery Awards," Kelly said.

"You were ironing your shirt then, so your creases stood out, just like Mike's."

"I know. Some things never change. But then again, this time we're going to Yarralumla, not Government House in Sydney!"

"Yes, a major step up. You're in the big league now. You're no longer just a Venturer but a piece of national asset."

Scott stopped ironing and took in what his mother said and agreed. He was being recognised as a piece of the Australian tapestry by the Queen's representative. Someone all young Australians could look up to.

"Of course, I didn't have crutches in Sydney for that ceremony."

"No, you didn't. But then again you hadn't completed a double rescue in the same day in arduous and trying circumstances."

"Okay touché."

The Morrows drove to Yarralumla which was about ten minutes away in the heart of Canberra. They were met at the gates by security guards who ushered them to a special parking area for guests. Yarralumla was magnificent. It had a long history and had been built and added to for more than a century so only parts of its original foundations remained. Large sweeping verandahs provided shade from the hot Canberra sun in summer for the Governor General, his wife and family or official guests. The Morrows made their way into an ante room where a lot of other bravery awardees and their families had gathered and were talking. Ten minutes later, an aide to the Governor General asked everyone to be seated. A bank of TV cameras was situated on the side of the room at the front with a gaggle of reporters.

Instinctively, Scott scanned the pack of Reporters. Mike had watched the Morrows enter the room and stood to the side when he saw Scott scanning the pack. Mike gave Scott the thumbs up, and the boy smiled broadly when he saw his Venturer Leader, albeit in his Journalist role.

One by one the awardees were called before the Governor General to receive their special accolade. Polite applause followed each presentation. Scott was called forward and the aide read out the special citation accompanying his accolade. Everyone in the room stood and clapped and broke with tradition. Governor General Monte Brereton was not surprised at the reaction. He had followed Scott's Media interviews since he took on the Russian Mafia and won. He too broke out in applause. Scott didn't know what to do. He was standing a pace back from the Governor General. Mike got Scott's attention and gave him the scout salute. He then closed his right hand and used his index and middle fingers like a pair of legs and moved his arm forward. Scott got the hint. The youth saluted the Governor General, turned, and marched back to his seat. The commotion died down amid a lot of people reaching forward to Scott to shake his hand as he tried to sit down.

Scott went with his parents to the verandah to enjoy a cup of tea with the Governor General. The Media sought Scott out and asked him to give a statement. Governor General Brereton saw the Media scrum starting to surround Scott and went to the youth's aid. He made a statement to the Media and congratulated Scott on becoming the country's first Young Citizen of the Year. Scott made a few statements, and the interviews were over.

The Governor General put his arm around Scott and walked off along the verandah with him to have a private word.

"Scott, I have been watching your progress since last year and have been most impressed. The way you dealt with the Russian Mafia was nothing short of spectacular for someone of your age.

"When I read your story of starting the national Rover Emergency Rescue Service, I was quite impressed. Then, when news broke of you being involved in Brett's rescue and saving the Rover on the same day, the feeling for you around the country went through the roof.

"The Prime Minister and I are old friends, and we have a regular chat about a lot of things. He too had been following your progress. When he saw you were trapped in a tree, he went out on a limb himself, so to speak, by authorising the Blackhawk helicopter."

"Sir, I never asked for any of this. I just did what had to be done."

"I know. That's what so fantastic about you. You are not out for self aggrandisement or publicity. In fact, I'm told you shy away from the Media if you can. I want you to make me a promise Scott."

"Sir, I'm at your service."

"Scott, I want you to promise me to keep working hard to learn more skills and then continue to place them at the disposal of the community as you have so far. Will you do that?"

"Excellency, that's the basis of a Queens Scout. I have always tried to maintain and fulfil the promise I made when I became a Venturer. I promise you I will continue to do that."

"Well done, Scott. I have a private message now from the Prime Minister. He has asked me to tell you if you ever need his help at a national level, to reach out and call him.

"I can tell you Scott, not every Prime Minister would ever say that to someone, especially through me as the Governor General."

Scott was now flummoxed. He didn't know what to say. A few moments of silence took place.

"Excellency, I want you to know I really appreciate what you and Prime Minister Anthony have passed on to me today. I am very humbled by what you both have said. I have never been treated this way by anyone in such high places. I will give you my solemn promise I will do my best to do my duty as and when it falls."

"Good Scott. Good."

The Governor General shook Scott's hand and parted company to be with his other guests. Scott stood in silence with a huge smile on his face as he took in what the Governor General had said to him.

The Morrows and Mike caught up with Scott after the Governor General moved on. Mike saw a huge change in Scott and was keen to know what had transpired. Scott asked the trio to walk with him through the gardens so he could tell them in private what had just happened. The youth was quite adept at walking with the aid of his crutches now and had no trouble over the loose pebbles on the walkway next to the verandah.

"Scott that is absolutely fantastic," Allan said.

"Trouble is, you have been subjected to another private conversation so none of this must ever be said publicly."

"I know, I know. But how fantastic the Governor General takes me aside and asks me to make him a promise. Then for him to tell me the Prime Minister will help me with anything I need if I get into trouble is anyone's dream. I'm just lucky."

"No Scott. I'd say you are blessed," Kelly said.

Allan's mobile phone rang, and he stepped away from the

trio to take the call. His face broadened into a huge smile, and he rang off. Scott watched his father with some amusement. He thought some funny work matter had been relayed to him.

"Scott, your mother and I have surprise for you we've been keeping from you," Allan said. "We want you to come with us and check out the Australian Rover Emergency Rescue Service just up the road."

"Dad, this is not a Media event, is it? Please say no."

"No. This is a private tour of the facility you helped start. Mike, will you join us please?"

"Thanks Allan. I've filed the story on the ceremony already, made up my quotes from Scott. I'm fine thanks."

"Typical reporter," Scott said.

The Morrows and Mike got into their respective cars and headed to the centre of the city, a few minutes up the road. Allan found the Rover Emergency Rescue Service headquarters easily enough; it was parking that was hard to find. Mike had the same problem. Eventually, they found a car parking area. The four linked up and walked to the rescue headquarters. When they entered the foyer a security guard asked them to wait while he summoned the Director in charge. A few moments later the lift doors opened and a middle-aged man in a suit stepped out.

"Hello Scott, Allan, and Kelly, I'm Aaron Wayte, the director of this emergency service. You must be Mike Hunter, welcome.

"Scott don't be annoyed with your father but he and I have been tic tacking by phone to find a suitable time when you could come down and have a look around.

"We figured you'd like to see how we run the area that swung into action to effect Brett's and your rescue."

Scott was impressed with his father. He had risen in his estimations a hundred-fold. Even Mike was taken aback by what was unfolding.

"Scott, we operate from the third floor and the people there would love to meet you in person. Then, I thought we could have a bite to eat before you head back to Sydney."

"This is pretty cool. Thank you. Sitting in a tree making a mobile phone call and sending a text message to an imaginary place is one thing. Visiting the real thing and meeting the people behind the scenes, is another."

Aaron pushed the lift button and ushered the group into the lift. A few seconds later the lift door opened onto a secure glass door foyer. Aaron took out his security card, pushed it into a slot and the main door opened. The group entered the room and was met by a young Rover.

"Hi Scott, I'm Ben Wolfe and I've been wanting to meet you for some time.

"I'm the Rover that manned the operations centre on Alexander Plateau when you were stuck in that tree with Brett. I'm also the same Rover that held back the Media while you and your parents escaped from the plateau when Tiny Tom brought you out."

Scott went pale. He was now embarrassed and had nowhere to go. The youth looked at Mike and then rallied.

"Ben, I was sort of out to it when I made it to the Alexander Plateau car park. But I was sure as hell glad you helped out the way you did and gave me protection. Thank you."

Scott then leaned forward on his crutches and shook Ben's left hand. Ben put his arm around Scott's shoulder and gave him a hug.

"Mate, we work together as a family. Anyway, now you are an honorary Rover we are really family.

"Well, at least in a scouting sense."

Scott and Ben both laughed. Aaron ushered the group into the main operations room and explained how it worked. He showed Scott and his parents and Mike around the emergency centre.

"Now, we've been through here and you've seen how it all works, we need to go back to the front door again," Aaron said.

"What for?" Scott asked.

"I've got something I need you to do for me."

Scott was puzzled but moved as quickly as his crutches could take him back to the front door. It was different. A crowd of people had gathered from behind their desks and spilled out to the foyer area. Scott was engaged in conversation with his back to the entrance. Aaron gave the signal and all conversation stopped. Scott turned around to see a giant ribbon had been placed across the security glass doors. Aaron was now holding a giant pair of scissors.

"Scott our ruse is over," Aaron said. "We know how much you don't like publicity, even though it follows your exploits. Today, however, is different. The only Media here is Mike Hunter, and we have a special task we want you to perform."

Scott looked at both his parents and then to Mike. His parents were smiling, and Mike lifted up a camera to take some photos.

Aaron continued: "Will you cut this beautiful ribbon and officially open the Scott Morrow Operations Room?"

Scott was taken back and almost collapsed. He looked at his father who shrugged. His mother smiled and Mike gave him the thumbs up. Scott drew a deep breath. He knew when he was beaten.

"It would be a pleasure and an honour," Scott said.

Aaron gave Scott the giant scissors and smiled. Scott positioned the scissors around the ribbon and smiled broadly and began to cut slowly through it while Mike took a series of photos.

"I hereby officially open the Scott Morrow Operations Room and wish all those who work here God's blessing as they help those less fortunate than themselves."

Scott then cut through the ribbon and loud clapping erupted as the glass doors automatically opened. Ben asked Scott to re-enter the room and check it out. The Venturer hobbled forward and noticed some flower garlands hanging in the operations room. On the centre wall was a poster of Scott and a large, engraved plaque under it. Scott was now trembling. He made his way to the poster and read the plaque.

'Scott Morrow Operations Room.'

Scott Morrow – Australia's first Young Citizen of the Year.

Tears came to Scott's eyes as he read and re-read the plaque. He was humbled.

"Thank you for all your support. Thank you."

Ben took the lead.

"Scott, we've all admired your energy in having this Australian Rover Emergency Rescue Service set up.

"It took a lot of clout to make it happen. It also took a special rescue that captured the notice of the nation – yours.

"When we knew and verified you were in trouble and needed help the call went out to Rover Crews across the State. We were inundated with offers for help. This translated into hundreds of Rovers racing to the Alexander Plateau.

"Do you realise the headache you caused by just doing the right thing and notifying us of your plight? Mate, we had so many offers of help our switchboard went into virtual meltdown. We had to call on Emergency Management Australia for help."

"I didn't know. I'm sorry," Scott said, feeling emotional.

Ben reached forward and put his arm on Scott's shoulder.

"Mate you did nothing wrong. You did everything right. In fact, you became the model we have now started to embody in our advertising. Not using your name of course, just your attributes.

"Let me tell you Scott, you have so many Rover Crews that want you as a member it is not funny. Behind the scenes we have managed to look after more than 200 enquiries for your membership.

"The way around all this and the way to take the heat off you was to make you an honorary Rover. That's why Bruce saw you in hospital after the PM visited and gave you a special scarf – the same one the PM was given."

Scott sat down. He had had enough. Mike stood next to him and placed his hand on his shoulder. Aaron took over.

"I think you've seen enough. It must be time for lunch," Aaron said as he winked at Scott.

Scott stood with moistened eyes.

"Ben thanks for all your great support. I mean it. It's not every day a Venturer has a Rover as a guardian angel. Thank you to everyone here also for the great support you not only gave me but the support you continue to give all those who fall prey to misadventure."

The operations room staff burst into applause. Ben started it and the rest of the staff helped him give Scott a B-R-A-V-O-O-O. Scott replied with a T-A-R. His father took control and started ushering Scott towards the lift again.

Lunch was a quick affair as Scott really wasn't that hungry. He had undergone too much today. Too many things of significance had occurred and each one was a special event for him.

Aaron asked him what sort of adventure he wanted to do next.

"I know I won't be canyoning anytime soon. I think I'll take up an offer Cameron made me of going scuba diving with him. You can't get into too much trouble there."

"You'll have a ball under the surface."

After lunch Allan and Scott thanked Aaron for what he and his staff had done. They walked out of the emergency headquarters building and back to their car. Mike was with them all the way and had found his car again.

The trip was now over for Scott. The canyon rescue drama had played out to its last event. Scott closed his eyes as he sat in the rear of his parent's car and tried to sleep.

"Now it is over. I'm free again," Scott thought.

He was right. Well, until the next adventure.

Author's Note

In Australia the emergency telephone number is Triple Zero ('000') to be in touch with Police, Ambulance, Fire and Rescue and the State Emergency Services.

Since *Canyon* was first published in 2008, Australia's Triple Zero Awareness Working Group, a combination of Federal and State Government representatives, developed a smartphone application for iOS and Android devices to:

- provide the caller with information about when to call Triple Zero, and
- provide the caller with information about who to call in various non-emergency situations.

 The app is called Emergency + and is available free through iTunes and Google Play Stores.

The only way of contacting Triple Zero (000) is with a voice call — you cannot use SMS, email, instant messaging, video calling or social media to contact emergency services via Triple Zero (000).

Apps are not able to automatically provide details of your location to Triple Zero (000) or an emergency service organisation — however, you can read out your GPS coordinates to the emergency operator if they are provided on your smartphone.

You should not rely on any smartphone app as your only way of requesting emergency assistance. In an emergency it is always best to call Triple Zero (000) direct.

However, Triple Zero Awareness Working Group has started working on ways to for users of the 000 emergency telephone number to also be used by SMS if required.

For more information go to:

www.triplezero.gov.au

About the Author

 Christopher J. Holcroft is the author of six books. His background is in communications, media training, complex public information planning and implementation, and journalism.

He was a member of the Australian Army Reserve for more than 43 years. His overseas deployments have included Bougainville (1999), East Timor (2001), and Iraq (2006).

For more than 36 years, Christopher has been involved in scouting, including Venturer Scout Units in both Victoria and NSW. Christopher was presented the Silver Wattle Award by Scouts Australia in August 2008 for his outstanding service to Scouting. He was later awarded the Silver Koala in 2016 for his distinguished service.

Christopher holds a Masters degree in Organisational Communication from Charles Sturt University and a Bachelor of Arts degree from the University of Technology, Sydney, where he majored in Journalism and Communications Technology. He is also a Justice of the Peace.

He is married to Yvonne and the couple has three sons. They live in NSW and enjoy outdoor recreational activities including camping, abseiling and scuba diving.